RIVER OF GLASS

DEBORAH BERGMAN

RIVER OF GLASS

G. P. PUTNAM'S SONS
New York

FOR ALL THE "G."S

Published by G. P. Putnam's Sons,
200 Madison Avenue, New York, NY 10016.
Published simultaneously in Canada

The text of this book is set in Bembo.

Library of Congress Cataloging-in-Publication Data

Bergman, Deborah.
River of glass/Deborah Bergman.
p. cm.
ISBN 0-399-13533-2
I. Title.
PS3552.E71934R58   1990   89-48520 CIP
813'.54—dc20

Printed in the United States of America
1 2 3 4 5 6 7 8 9 10

This book has been printed on acid-free paper.

PART I

◇

THE
SOUTHERN
CROSS

CHAPTER ONE

◇

They tell me it's too dangerous to do by myself. I tell them I don't know any other way to do it. Not anymore. Outside of the sun, hot molten glass is the brightest thing you ever saw. But it seems like every time I dip my blowing iron into the furnace to add a new gather to my shape, behind me a man is casting a shadow.

Some of these men I know, some I don't. Six or seven use this studio. Usually whoever he is, he stays silent. And today like every day, the stillness his darkness casts across the furnace light tells me he's only waiting for me to hurt myself.

I step closer to the mouth of the oven. Almost instantly, the bandanna around my forehead goes wet. I begin to wind the gather onto the pipe by feel because up here, even from behind the dark glasses, I have to look away from the bright crucible. If I step any closer, the heat might melt my face smooth. And even though a glass oven hisses, when I get this close I hear a roar.

Behind me I can hear him stirring, and his shadow, at my feet now, grows longer: he's taken a few steps away. I keep turning the iron to wind more glass onto its tip. Then I lift the iron out of the kiln and away, so the shadow with eyes can clearly see the rod is almost as tall as I am. I roll it, back and forth, back and forth, so the tender bud of glass on the end will not fall. By myself, I carry the bud back to the bench and give it skin with steam and grow it with my breath.

I can feel his disappointment when the shape sets in and heat and weight have not undone me.

But when he walks away, he does not take his shadow with him. I find it trapped and dancing in my glass.

◊

At dinner, I tell Javier. Not the part about the shadow. I hate that shadow, but it means something to me too, and I don't want him to laugh that part away. Instead, I tell him how they watch me. How they offer to marver for me if I will just tell them what shape I want, how they point out that they would be happy to help me add color to what I am making by holding the punty above my shape as I turn and guide it so other lines of glass will drip down and span it, neat as penmanship, like two strong hands spanning a waist. I remind Javier that right now, color doesn't interest me.

That's when he laughs. Clearly, he doesn't think color has anything to do with why I don't want help.

When the women come into the studio, I observe, they leave me alone.

Javier stops laughing. "Whatever's wrong, Tess," he

says, "you're not going to solve it with a bunch of women."

That stings. Javier and I only cross paths a few times a week at most. Sometimes, only twice a month. Yet no matter how long it's been or what's gone on, every time we see each other he makes me mad. And every minute we spend together I wonder what will happen next.

Now, for instance, I laugh too.

Across the wicker table, Javier's eyes brighten in the strong, still face. Over the few months we've known each other, I've rarely seen that face move. I've seen it crinkle, in laughter, and break open, in pain. And then reassemble itself again. But just move and stay itself, never. The eyes, live and light in the flushed dark skin, dart instead. I'm never sure what color they are. I just know they can flare and recede like my furnace's gas flames and that, without really having thought about why, I assume they're just as potent.

Javier is taller than my idea of a wrestler, but he's built the same. In this seaside town of slender limbs, his substance stands out. I cannot decide whether I think he's attractive. For me, he's a new idea of a man. When we're together, I can barely stop looking at him for trying to figure it out.

"I want to show you the studio." I purposely change the subject.

"I have a little time," he agrees. When Javier and I are together neither of us say yes, and neither of us say no. But things happen anyway.

We leave our coffee without paying. Javier owns this restaurant. I wait on the curb, studying the sea, slate-colored in this light, while he stops to talk with some other Argentines at a nearby table. It's impossible to tell whether they're chatting or making plans: I've learned that where Argentines in Begar, Spain, are concerned, both are complicated. The men at the table, dressed much more appropriately in shorts and loose, thin shirts than Javier in his habitual heavy boots and jeans, occasionally flick their eyes in my direction. They probably wonder whether I'm Javier's girlfriend. This kind of thing happens to me often. I'm the sort of soft, even-featured person, not too light and not too dark, whom people naturally relate to my companion when I have one. I often get taken for a sister, a girlfriend, a daughter. This is ironic, because I try so hard to relate myself to no one. To be related to no one and see what happens next is one of the reasons I've stopped here in Begar.

Javier is touching the shoulder of one man and the other three are looking intently at him. Above the dark beard the eyes have dimmed. Javier is completely indifferent to the fact that while everyone else on the terrace has taken great pains to uncover as much skin as possible in the balmy evening air, he has gone to the other extreme. I realize that with the bandanna still on my head and the pigment-covered smock, I alone come close. Even so, Javier and his acquaintances look like they go together, while I, no matter how related I may look to Javier from the perspective of others, stand out alone. From the table rise the operatic rhythms of Argentine Spanish that make everything sound like melodrama until you get used to them. I still haven't. I always wonder if Javier and his friends truly don't hear the melodrama coursing through their words, or if it's just that to them it's as basic to speech as grammar.

As he approaches, I wonder if taking Javier to the studio is such a good idea. I don't know him that well, and this time of night we may be alone at the studio. I don't want to suggest an intimacy I don't feel.

"No one here wants to hurt you," he says firmly, placing one hand on my shoulder. "Everyone here is your friend."

I lead him up away from the sea. I feel both safe and chastened.

As we make our way through the narrow street filled with butchers, bakers, jewelers, and tourist bars, I look down to the end of each cross street for its glimpse of the sea. Javier and I have always met on the waterfront, where everything is open and simple. That's his turf, and mine. Back here, life is messier. You get pushed up on the sidewalks. You have to say excuse me. You have to say hello. I notice, as we walk along, that back here I am the one who has many acquaintances, women who sell me my hand lotion, my bread, and my espadrille shoes, while Javier has none. Tonight after each woman greets me, her eyes drop and soften, and she runs on quickly, more quickly than usual. There is something to this routine, which I observe several times, of both the obedient servant and the frightened mother.

I have been in this town since spring and this has never happened before. I look over at Javier, who pretends not to notice, but who has become more solicitous with each encounter.

Certain names float behind South Americans who have come to live in Spain: *hippi, mafioso, ladrón.* On Sundays, you can see these words and ones like them play across the faces of the local people as they promenade slowly and at a safe distance from the tables of beautiful young South Americans selling papier-mâché harlequin jewelry and bumming cigarettes. Only the disenfranchised, like me, come closer. The sad, self-conscious expressions on these faces remind me of mine. I know that in the early nineteen eighties Argentines and Chileans come to Spain because they think it may be easier here: to stay alive, or to start life over again, or both.

People come for both reasons. So you learn quickly not to ask them where they come from, or why they're here, because the answers you get are angry and vague. But you know anyway. It's odd to think of nice middle-class kids like you being plucked out of bed, taken away. Of more of the same kind of kids, terrified, cornered, taking up guns. Of others, disappearing abroad to escape both fates, and still others stepping through the crack that's opened up in the world just to drift through it and its terror and its power for no reason but to become larger than a child. *Hippi, mafioso, ladrón.* Until right now, when I've heard those names I've never thought of Javier.

I try not to look at him until I'm sure the connection I've just made is not registering on my face, but I can't help myself. Luckily, it doesn't matter, because just at that moment he's found an acquaintance of his own: a policeman. The greetings they exchange are very polite, even affectionate. This is the elderly gentleman who tickets the cars parked between Javier's restaurant and the ocean, and therefore they share certain interests. But I notice that even though his voice soars with solicitude, Javier's face is even stiller and darker than usual and his eyes are on fire.

"Pardon me," I interject. The officer looks puzzled. "Please excuse me for robbing this gentleman from you." I look at my wrist, where there is no watch. "We're late for dinner."

Then I am closing the studio door behind us.

Just the two molten lights in penumbra: the furnace holding the crucible, and the annealing oven. No greeting but the hiss of gas. Javier looks surprised.

My bench, I say, pointing.

"Ah." He sits down nearby. "How did you know that?"

"What?"

"That I was losing my temper."

"No one here wants to hurt you." He shifts his weight on the bench as I tease him with his own words.

"Show me." He looks back. He's regained his composure, and his eyes are lively. It occurs to me that in Javier's life contentment may play a much more complicated role than it does in my own, it may be the gas jet regulator that keeps the flame turned down.

"Show you. Okay. Do you know what tempering is?"

He shakes his head no.

"After you give glass shape, you have to heat and cool it slowly. Like over there." In the annealing oven, the glass shapes, barely discernible from the endometrium of heat and light, glow more softly than the liquid glass in the furnace. But the way they seem to pull away from this pure heat and light into form is hypnotic. When I'm not here, I love to think of these glass shapes tempering. Nothing I know is more visibly poised between ideal and reality.

"They call that the glory hole," I tell Javier. We still haven't turned on the light. My voice is hushed but I can't help speaking quickly. I feel proud. "Glass isn't a solid. It's a liquid. So when it cools, it has surface tension, like water. The outside cools first, and then the insides pull away. There is even a way to look at the internal stresses. They're light and dark. Eventually, glass like that shatters. So what you do is heat it up so the insides and outsides reach the same temperature and then let it cool slowly. That dissolves the internal stress. No more surface tension: instead you have compression, which makes the glass strong." Javier is silent. "It doesn't matter what you make," I go on, "if you don't temper it. It won't stand up."

"Show me how to do it," Javier says after a while. His eyes move around, looking, no doubt, for the men I've described. I know from the light under the door that someone is in the back room, but I choose not to share this information. Javier's eyes rest on a stack of panes near my bench. I've been messing around with something new on them, but it hasn't crystallized.

"That's nothing," I tell Javier. "That's a window."

I choose a pipe and stand behind him as he dips for his gather. I blow the first breath for him, so he'll see how not to give too much air. And then I stand back and watch. His hands, small in proportion to the rest of him but just as strong, spin the iron gently but firmly. He's a more attentive learner than I would have imagined.

"That's enough," he protests eventually, and his eyes widen as I score the mouth of his shape and smack the iron sharply so it breaks off clean. Javier gives the form eyes, ears, and a tail. It's a little creature of the sort everyone seems to make on the first attempt; Javier's is predictably equine. Before I remove it to temper, he examines the shape carefully.

"Look at that." He points just below where the light catches what could be called the glass creature's chest. "If I stand right here I can see you inside, right under this curve. It looks like you're dancing," Javier says.

◇

A week later, I'm sliding off the walls. I know I'm running toward something: that's why I came here. The sight of the sea fills up every chink that gaps open in me, every hesitation, fear, or lack. In cafes on Sunday afternoons, promenaders order the splits and plastic saucer glasses of the plentiful local champagne as easily as soda. Spilled, it is not wasted, but holy: townspeople have shown me I have only to dip my fingers in it and anoint my forehead for luck. This is an approach to life I have decided to take to heart.

It's the abundance of that sea, and the glee of that champagne, and the taste of the smooth cured ham that kept me here. But today I can't feel or see or taste for the shadows. I'm all caught up in the current inside me. The sky is beautiful. From here in the dark, I can see kites on the beach but still I can't get out of bed. I've been up since dawn with the coup-de-grace cries of the Saturday-night revelers as they stagger home and, later, the scolds of mothers hurrying their children toward church. By now, it's about three. I am supposed to meet a buyer for one of the local shops but I can't haul myself to the street. I'm afraid I'll reveal my permeability and the carrion birds will see. The men in the studio will scare me, and I'll drop my iron. I'll lose my place. I'll hurt myself. *Here,* they'll say, *let me help you.* Afterward I'll feel defiled. I'll pick up and leave. I'll leave myself.

At this thought, I come up to the surface. Why is it, I wonder, that if I leave here, I'll leave me?

An hour later, I'm sipping coffee at Javier's restaurant.

He hasn't been in yet today, and the day manager says he's due anytime. He gestures at the phone on the counter next to him and recites Javier's home number, but I wave away the offer. I can't imagine speaking to

Javier on a telephone. I can't hear my voice, or his voice.
I can't imagine what we'd say. "Come back," says the
manager patiently. "Later today. Leave a note."

I am crossing the street in front of the officer issuing
parking tickets when I see my friend's car pull into an
illegal space. The officer smiles. Javier smiles. He gets
out slowly. I can see he's been horseback riding. Slowly,
he unloads a canvas bag onto the ground and stops to
examine the front door lock, which is sticking. He
hasn't seen me. "Ha!" he says when it opens, and I can
tell that fixing it makes him feel truly satisfied.

I'm jealous. It's so normal. In a year, I haven't touched
a steering wheel. I haven't cooked a meal. I go places
other people go, and do the things they're doing. I've
started working glass again, but only recently, and I'm
not sure it will stick. And that's all I do.

"Hi," I say.

He looks up. He says nothing. He nods over his
shoulder, and we go inside and sit down.

I choose my words carefully. I say, "I don't know if
maybe I didn't accidentally kill someone. I don't think
so, though."

"Back home, you mean," says Javier.

I nod.

"You didn't," he says definitively. When he looks at
me, there's a new twinkle in his eye: I want to know
the source of that humor. "You couldn't. You don't
have it in you. You're a good person. You're a little
lonely, and that makes you a little crazy, but you're not
mortally careless. You're not negligent." I start to speak,
but he shakes his head. "I'm a very good judge of people," Javier explains. And then, something happens that
I've never seen. This still face of his smiles open and
gently closes again, intact: no breaking open, no need

for recomposing. "I know," he emphasizes slowly, "the sort of person who kills."

"That's something," I say, "you found out about in Argentina." He looks at me again, and the humor in his eyes is so strong now, and so affectionate, it's almost palpable. But this amusement is not a reaction to what I've said but directed toward the careful stillness I have borrowed from him and, which, I myself acknowledge, barely masks my galloping curiosity.

"It's quite easy to kill," says Javier Puig.

◇

On the beach, at night, under the stars, men talk more. If I stay quiet, I learn a lot about what they regret, and what they admire, and what they want.

Javier's friends never asked me to the water to watch the sunset with them until they saw me leave the restaurant with him the day we went to the studio, but that could be coincidence. Javier himself always has business to attend to when someone decides it's time to go to the beach. But, to my surprise, I've found that fading into the black while strangers talk is deeply comforting to me, the way swimming in saltwater comforts the body whose basic substance it so closely resembles. I'm not sure which substance of mine it is that has found its element here on the waterfront. I do know I'll keep coming until I find out. I grab handfuls of cold sand as the men describe boats that travel under skies filled with constellations we don't see here. The longing is for clearness of water and deserted coves.

They are always tacking far out into the ocean under the Southern Cross, when the other talk begins. This other conversation, which always comes dark and in waves, crests just a little bit, one memory's worth at a time, and then subsides back into a deep sea of silence.

Its sentences remain unfinished: *Gregorio was in the airport when* . . . The expressions on their faces that follow these words say more: a grimace followed by a shake of the head that contains sorrow and distance and a perspective that seems learned, like the love that remains for a sibling who has gone bad and caused to many inexcusable pain. With more incredulity than anger, another voice chimes in: *two hundred people were killed and he just* . . .

No one says so, but I know that what is being recalled is a day when the homecoming of a hero, who all hoped would bring their country back from the brink of chaos, inspired a bloodbath before he'd even stepped out of the airport, instead. It was a day when for many hope collapsed into fear as easily as a major key progresses to a minor one; when the crisp line between loyalty and treason; bravery and crime began to dance and blur.

This part of the conversation always starts with the airport. That is the signal. This first signal is answered by a second, then a third, and soon all the chaos that's come since that nightmare began is swelling up and back again under the dreamed boat and under the real stars and tide. Who fought. Who didn't. Who lived. Who died. Who escaped completely unscathed. Who worked for the wrong side. Who was barely an adult, and who had barely been a child. How they got from there to here and why they did while others didn't is never mentioned aloud, although I can feel it being remembered. I wish Javier were here, because I trust his perspective the most. But he always stays away from these meetings.

And now, it is as if with the ripples of spoken memory they are telling each other about who is in town from home, and what side each person was on, and which of many sad events each might have been soiled by, or escaped from, or been drawn into there. The words they speak, which imply but do not spell out, are like flashes of phosphorus on the dark tide. I can't tell if their reticence is for my benefit or theirs. I don't dare to ask more, but I am intensely curious. There is a sense of something building, that sharing all this information from the past does more than merely help them get more smoothly from day to day or cleanse old pain. But one thing I notice is, these men seem to have no politics now. Their vision is sailing: alone. No country. No company. Just them, and the stars.

Whenever I think of that, I feel cold.

It is almost impossible to ignore the fact that by now I seem to know some little snippet of information about the past of each one of them except Javier.

That makes me feel even colder.

One night I hear: "Those kids Javier took up on the mountain, does anyone even know who made it out except for him?"

"Shhhh," comes a voice, and all eyes turn to me.

◇

The hurricane lamps sell best. I try goblets, they're easier, they're less expensive. No one wants them. I ask Marisol, who sells shampoo. I just point in a shop window and ask, what do you think? I don't tell her who made it. She thinks a long minute. Then she says, "It's pretty. It's interesting. But I wouldn't want to drink from it." Why, I wonder, looking with her. We both stand there pressed up against the window, examining the curves of this long-bowled goblet while behind us the sandy crowd mills up the cross streets. "Well," she says finally, "the color. It's as if anything you drank from it would taste bitter. That red brown on the bottom. Like a river going dry."

Then she spies one of the hurricane lamps, shot through with the lightest spiral of cobalt and stars. A globe at the center, and tapering up gradually to the top so you can cup your hands around the lip and feel the candle dancing inside.

"Ah," says Marisol. "Now that, I could drink from."

◊

I still wonder, how did his letter get all the way here from another continent so quickly, just after I got a mailing address again? Among the other things he wrote was, *I forgive you,* words which, of course, carry inside them that other message, *I find you guilty.*

I found a way to make it okay: I decided receiving letters like this one is simply part of being still. And it is time for me to be still. For a year, it was right to be in motion. It got me going, it ran the light through me, it made me bright and made me clean. But that time has passed. If I start again now, it would be running away instead of running toward. So when I got the letter I remembered I knew a way to keep moving, even while I stayed still.

That way was working glass.

I was lucky. There was a studio right in town.

My first day at this studio I wondered, if I added this piece of paper, this letter, to the glass batch, what would happen? Would it disintegrate, marry the clear stuff, grow to a new shape I willed with my breath? I toyed with the chemical influences of paper and ink. What colors would this piece of paper shade my mix? The green iron imparts? The violet of manganese? Or, what if I simply unrolled it like wallpaper around a curved side that was still cooling but already solid? Would it burn?

Then one day on the beach when I wasn't paying attention, it must have fallen out of my bag and into the sand, because when I got home it was gone.

It's funny how life has a way of taking care of these things.

"Tell me why you came here again?" Javier asks, although we both know quite well I've never mentioned it. I've brought him his little horse creature, now cooled and solid. He holds it in his hand, then gestures over his shoulder toward the ocean. I follow him, and he leads me to his car. He puts the horse on the dashboard, in the center.

"It'll slide and fall," I warn.

He picks it up and tests the weight in one hand, looking at me. Then he puts it in the middle of the backseat.

"One of those cupholders with the stickpads on the bottom." The tone of his voice is mild, but his eyes seem to flash with irritation. It is only then that I understand that perhaps he is trying to say something by putting the horse there, on the dashboard. I wish I knew what it was. But maybe I do.

I have learned that I am a reactive person. That's why it was so good to run free, alone: put me with people and I creep back in the shadows. I guess that's another reason I like glass. Glass is a reactive material. It responds to me. Without me, it's nothing.

I look at Javier now and I see someone who has made choices and acted on them. The shape he's blown out of his life is his. Whereas I am a bowl, that with a touch can shatter.

"I came here to do something." This is the true answer to his first question.

"Do something? What?"

"I'm not sure exactly. Whatever it is I'm supposed to do."

◇

On Sunday, the newspaper magazine runs a photograph of a field nestled in the hills of Central America
that is littered with human bones and skulls.

I'm drawn. The marriage of spareness and curve that
is bone is one I find particularly enticing. But then, I'm
trained to look under the story and into the shape. For
a few minutes I'm like a camera, shifting my conscious-
ness back and forth from the horror to the beauty in
search of the optimal aperture of understanding. There
isn't one. There's no place to rest. There's nothing to
do but keep moving from one to the other, back and
forth.

If I lived in a place where teenagers ended up in fields
like these perhaps as often as they are accepted to college I, too, would look for a way to channel that rest-
lessness. That seasick pull between the pain of an
unimagined life and the quietly imagined repose of the
soul. I, too, might end up testing the space between
patriotism and disobedience, or patriotism and crime.
These skulls are not from the countries my new friends
have come from. The evidence from those places is still
what doctors would call anecdotal: Among it, reports
of drugged young people dumped from helicopters into
churning sea; of imperfectly healed scars in the earth
like this one, opened wide on front pages so others can
look within.

Later, at the market, I look closely at the faces of the
young South Americans peddling stars and hearts. It's
not just their coloring, or the bones, which echo North
American more often than I might have expected them
to before I got here. It's an attitude to the world, an
expression in the eyes. A particular balance between re-
sentment and confidence. A poise that says they're sim-

ply humoring their circumstances, but a sadness that says they might be humoring them for a long time.

I still cannot shake the feeling that we hold something in common.

For days, I go nowhere near the studio or Javier.

◊

Instead, I go to the beach.

I settle on a quiet cove sheltered by a cliff. During siesta, between two and five, the shop people come here, and so do other women from the North. After a day or two of feeling invisible I realize now that eyes are following me with mildly approving glances. Not necessarily sexual, just aesthetic. At home at night I study myself in the mirror, trying to understand what they see. Trying to imagine how it was that they feel pleasure in the way I am leaded together.

The local people don't talk much near the water. They swim instead. The silence with which they come and go from my side is unnerving. One minute, two long bodies flank me. The next sound I hear is a soft splash cleaving the silence like sheetglass breaking. If I follow the sound with my eyes I can find one of the bodies I'd thought was still lying next to me knee-deep in blue water. From twenty feet away, on this expanse of sand, against this smooth sea, each person loses individuality and simplifies into a form.

This cove doesn't deepen quickly, and the way the clear shallow water gathers and reflects sunlight makes flesh look soft. It's a visual acid. As I watch each swimmer, I find myself considering the bone beneath. I want to get down to essentials. It's easy to do this on a beach: no one is watching you, so my observations go unchecked.

Then, I too go to swim. And I'm surprised at how

cool and soft I feel down at that place that seems to
reduce everything to its most common denominator,
how waves lap by like doves.

Back on the beach, I hover between sleep and wake-
fulness.

Pieces of cut glass ready to be leaded into a stained
glass window float on a tide, which widens out to a
sea. Treading water is another bearded man, younger
than Javier. I float, I'm a fish, I'm a cat, I'm any sun-
loving creature. I give myself up.

"You turn a very pretty color in the sun," a voice
says somewhere above me.

◇

I'm on my way back from a late counter supper of barbecued chicken and cheap champagne when I run into
Carmen, who lives down the street. She asks me if I
want to go along with her and her boyfriend to Ilium,
an open-air club on a sandy cove. I haven't been since
I joined the glass studio, but I know I haven't signed
up for any time this week. I can't go back there until I
stop thinking about the skulls.

But that will be happening soon; underneath I feel
new and smooth. So twenty minutes later she and I are
sipping screwdrivers above a sunken stone dance floor
packed with friends and strangers. The dancers are edgy
with the electricity of the coming squall.

It has been a long time since I've gone dancing. Small
puddles of alcohol gleam on the floor, and the sounds
of Catalan, Spanish, German, and English blend around
me. Soon the beat wins me over. Every once in a while
I look up and see lightning flash through the sky. No
one pays the least bit of attention. I dance for a long
time, stopping once in a while to rest on the steps. People from the beach join me, then move away. Carmen
is a relentless dancer, and I want very much to keep up

with her. Turning, I see Javier standing on a banquette near the bar. He waves at me. I wave back. I turn away. Needles of cool water begin to fall on my arms. I don't want to be tired, but suddenly, I don't want to be wet at all.

"Tessa! Come on over here!" Javier is standing at the bar and he's waving. The dance floor is still fairly crowded despite the storm, and the local people are retreating under awnings to watch the ever more elaborate movements of the tourists left on the dance floor.

"I was watching you," Javier informs me.

"And what did you see?"

He shrugs and gestures at the dancers.

"Why haven't I seen you lately, anyway?"

"I've been in the sun." On the horizon, dawn is lighting the clouds pink. I'm tired and I'm not tired.

"Have you had enough of this?" he asks.

I feel happy someone cares how I feel. The last of the mood of the past two weeks evaporates. I feel physically lighter, more agile, more responsive. I feel like I've shed a skin.

"Let's go," Javier says.

◇

The glass horse is back on the dashboard, steadied by a little stand.

Watching him carefully, I get in. I'm level-headed, and have found that this enables me to go more or less wherever I want to. It's a myth that level-headed people have less fun in life. It pays off.

We're halfway back to town and the rain is stopping. Light is cleansing the clouds from the sky, and for the next fifteen minutes the world will look as though we are seeing it through a chip of bottle-green glass. Far out in the sea, a single motorboat with a water-skier behind knifes the aquamarine. Without warning, Javier turns off the main road. I turn my head toward him in question. He just grins.

This road ends in a stable of a dozen stalls curled around a muddy field. A boy is exercising a fat white pony in a dilapidated ring.

Without speaking, Javier stops the car and walks through the mud to a big bay with a bandaged eye. When he's examined the eye he leaves the bay and moves from stall to stall, crooning.

"This is my family," Javier calls back to me. "We are five. Come meet them."

He moves back to the bandaged bay and I watch him hold its head and gently examine the injury, clucking.

I'm still tired and not tired. There's that special intimacy with the world you feel watching dawn come to it, and that gives confidence. In my new skin, I am going to do something. I consider my high-heeled sandals and flimsy cotton trousers. Village clothes. Dancing clothes.

"I haven't been on a horse since I was thirteen," I call.

"So who's asking you?"

"You are. Aren't you?"

Shaking his head, he turns around. He looks as if he has just enjoyed a private joke. "I was just going to introduce you, but well, fine, we can ride."

Mount from the left, never the right I chant from deep memory. And then I am in the saddle of a roan mare. But as I try to find my seat Javier mounts his bay and my horse follows his away from the stables, over a rise, and down a fountain of red rocks. We're alone in the field. In Begar, all attention is directed toward the sea or the hills, which leaves this strip of prickly humming land unnoticed in between. The green sky and a light breeze light the whole landscape with a feeling of mysterious preanimation. For a moment, we watch the land move.

"Anda, ya," Javier says suddenly.

Both horses break into a trot. I try to rein in the mare but it's useless.

"I like to exercise them every day, if I can," he calls, without looking back.

"How far do these trails go?" I am already out of breath.

"All the way up the hills." He sits back loosely in his saddle, pivots to take me in, and grins. "You okay?"

"I don't mind the pace, if that's what you mean."

"I can see that." He turns back again, and I wonder if it is to hide another smile. "Sometimes I come out here and spend three or four days alone. Sleep in the field." He gestures, introducing me to the whole landscape. "I don't really like people."

"Come on. I see how well you treat people."

"Money. New business. That's what I do, start businesses."

"You don't talk to me to start businesses."

"Do you miss your country?" Javier asks.

"I don't know. I don't have family there, my mother owns one of those gourmet barges for American tourists that does the canals in France. I don't keep up with many friends, either." I pause. "And you?"

"I was a gambler. My mother threw me out on my ear. For a while I raised horses and traveled, all over the world. Then I came here."

The tone of his voice says that, at the very least, this is only a small part of the truth. It also says he's confident I'm aware of this.

"Relax," he suggests. "The horse is gentle. Don't be afraid."

"Are you trying to scare me?"

"Are you scared?"

"Are you?"

Now when he looks at me his eyes are gleaming and his face is very still.

"I have a special invitation for you. Come to my house and watch me shave off my beard. Then I will take you home."

I search for some visual clue that will give me information I find myself unable to request in words.

The grin is back.

"For a passport. You can be the witness." Then he canters away, leaving me to watch.

◇

We rest against the white door while Javier finds his house key, then I am moving through the darkness inside. I have never been to Javier's apartment. It has a familiar, close scent, neither pleasant nor unpleasant. It's the scent of the places people live in but do not call their homes.

"How were you going to get home from that club, anyway?" Javier calls from the door.

"I don't know. Um, I guess the boyfriend of the girl I came up with. That's how I got there."

"Oh. And your boyfriends, Tessa?"

"Oh, I don't know. What about yours?" Far away, lightning begins to flash again softly.

"Sexually, I am satisfied. In my business, I am satisfied. But I get very violent, very crazy."

Electric light blazes. A rough plaid spread covers the couch next to me. The grayish walls are bare except for a few snapshots taped up above a lone bookshelf. It's a sad room. We all live year-round in beach rentals intended for tourists in high season, but this is the first one I have been in where nothing has been done to disguise this fact. A large console television stands in the room's center.

Javier picks up a small, covered silver can and places it on the sink.

"The new house isn't ready yet," he explains. "Come and watch me damage my face." In the bathroom I hear water running.

I don't want to join him quite yet. I stop to look at the snapshots. The first one is one of a girl who is either a mature teenager or a young-looking college student. She has a nice smile and lots of thick, reddish-brown hair.

If I draw the curtains, the room will fill with daylight. But this is not my apartment, so I join Javier at the door of the bathroom where in front of the mirror he is snipping at his beard with an old pair of scissors. His small, thick hands hover uncertainly as he cuts from one side and then the other, high and then low. He bends close to his reflection as he cuts and he is murmuring. "Ay! How I am going to damage my face!" over and over again like a little song. The single fluorescent bulb has sucked all the color from his head and shoulders. Even the gas flame in his eyes is turned low. The room is filling with steam.

In the mirror he looks at me.

I look into the bedroom. I make out a white shirt thrown over a chair and two unmade single beds.

"Do you know how to shave?" Javier asks. "The last time I shaved was to escape from Argentina. Then my brother did it for me." He grimaces as he touches a razor gently to his cheek.

"He shaved my head, too, I was bald! So there I was, disguised, ready to flee the country. But people came right up to me on the street and slapped me on the back, they said, *'Qué tal,* Javier, how are you?' " He works in a small circle, closing in on his jaw. *"Ay mi madre.* Outside I never really change."

I turn and rest my spine against the edge of the door. I want him to go on and I want him to stop. I don't know which I want more, and it must show, because Javier's reflection smiles knowingly at me from the mirror.

The lines of his new face are emerging. He looks younger, and more vulnerable. He's bleeding in several places, and now that this face is naked, I see its stillness disturbed by involuntary ripples of memory and concentration. He's still honing himself with his razor.

"You see, Tess? I look the same."

"Yes, Javier, you look the same."

As he emerges from the shower in a white robe, drying his face, I ask the question: "Why do you need to get rid of the beard for the passport?"

No ripples now. "For the picture. I must have a clean face. For a passport from my country." He pauses. "A false passport." Javier narrows his eyes at me and turns to the kitchenette. "I can offer only mate, *gringa.* Not even sugar. Willing to give it a try? Good, excellent!" He picks up the silver can he placed on the sink when we came in and empties it into the sink.

"Gringa, gringa. Do you miss your country, *gringa?"*

"Not particularly. I told you that before."

Water begins to simmer in the kettle.

"What is this *gringa* business?" I want to know. Outside, the wind is up again. Javier still hasn't opened the curtains. I want to know what the weather looks like outside.

"You know I only do it with tenderness."

The water begins to boil against the tin. Javier fills

the mate bulb with it and screws the lid on. Then he hands it to me. I suck on the metal straw. The liquid is green and bitter, like a thick tea. Javier puts both hands to his face. "How I have hurt myself," he repeats. He looks at me.

I reach the bottom of the mate and look for somewhere to put the bulb.

"Don't put it down. The bulb must never touch the table until the mate is finished."

I hand it back and he rises and fills it for himself. When he sits down again he looks at me.

"Do you think you will become old, Tessa?" he asks. I say I think I will.

"I won't," he announces. "I'll die young. You and I, Tessa, we are very lonely people. We are on the margins. That place you went to tonight. Everyone you know is at a place like that, but still it's always too loud to talk to them." The volume of his voice rises at this, as if that music reaches all the way here. "That's because they're tired of each other. It's always the same."

"This town isn't exactly what I'd call typical." I want to use that half-maternal, half-amused tone I've heard Marisol and Carmen use to counter their men, but my voice comes out neutral instead. Half of what he says is true, the other half is melodrama and whiskey talking. The combination embarrasses me. I don't know what to do to stop it.

Javier stands up and goes to the closet, pulling his bathrobe tighter around him. "Yes. It is. The whole world's this way."

To my amazement, he's come back from the closet pointing a small black pistol at his own head. He holds it sloppily and it shakes back and forth in his hand.

"You see this?" he demands. "I have to keep this in

my closet in case some lunatic from the Argentine police comes looking for me."

He points the gun at me. He doesn't move. The
muzzle shakes. I have no idea whether the pistol is
loaded.

"The whole world is crazy." He's almost pleading.
"When I was seventeen my *compañera,* the girl I loved,
was shot and killed in front of me. She was just fifteen.
Up in the hills."

The gun begins to tremble faster in his hand. I keep
looking at Javier and his gun. I decide that if I look at
the pistol hard enough, it won't go off.

"I had to leave my country," continues Javier, "and
now I am so accustomed to losing things I sleep in a
different bed every night so I won't get used to one."
He jerks his hand forward and over his head, and the
pistol slips through his fingers to the floor.

There is nothing to say.

"It's a crazy, crazy world," mumbles Javier. His face
has relaxed and regained its stillness.

I notice my hands and feet are cold. I feel nothing
but cold.

And then the rain comes back, strong. We both listen.
I'm wide awake. Every sense I have is alert, my soul is
singing. I could recite the periodic table, batch mixtures
for half a dozen different kinds of glass. I could cook
Javier a huge American breakfast, or learn to water-ski.
I could write a long letter home. I could ask Javier to
tell me why his girlfriend died. I could get it out of
him.

But I don't. Not now.

"I should go," I say. "The windows are open in my
apartment. Everything's going to be wet and cold. You
look very handsome without your beard."

"Stay here if you like, Tessa. There is plenty of room."

"No thanks. I'll be okay."

"Whatever you like."

I open the curtains wide. The blue-gray light of the rain-dancing sea fills the room.

Javier blinks.

I kiss him on the cheek and I go.

CHAPTER TWO

◇

A glass skull is not hard to make. I can build a model, drape the sheetglass over it, and bake them together in the kiln until heat forces the substance above to surrender to the shape below. I could fire the surface with enamel, or fuse glass on top, or both.

Instead, I dip a rod into liquid glass until some of it gathers around the tip. I partially coat this clear gather with another one that is gray, another that is blue. I am making a goblet the color of sea.

At least I've given the shadow boundaries now, even if they are only the boundaries of water.

I'm not at all sure how much longer I'll be doing this.

Plate glass is sometimes tempered with a treatment of jets of cool air that reverse the usual patterns of a cooling liquid. The glass cools in a way that brings compression to the skin of the sheet, and buries the surface tension deep inside. A sheet of glass tempered like this is very strong. It can be so strong you could lie on it if it were stretched out between two saw-horses.

Yet, one blow to one corner can cause the whole sheet to shudder into identical fractures. Think of the first ripple caused by a stone in a pond, and how the water responds with a second ripple, a third, and then so many you can't count them. It's the same way with plate glass. Glass is always a liquid, even when it looks solid. Even when it holds another liquid, even when it cuts you. Shattering glass is a different kind of wave.

There are clothes and newspapers all over the floor of the apartment I leased from May through September, and the white sheets on the unmade daybed are tangled beyond recognition. One is torn almost in half. I know my landlady will charge me for it by the inch, but I can't seem to get myself to bring it to her attention. On the table next to the blue vase of yellow flowers, hope: the meal I've prepared of two beautiful ripe peaches, a half baguette, a split of wine.

In the chink of sea visible between two white chimneys on the next street, sailboats coast by.

It's another Sunday. I want to do something. The beach will be too crowded. On Sunday, people who spend more than a week here usually stay home.

I kind of like this mess. It makes me feel safe, like I'm in a nest. I turn on the radio and eat my food slowly. Midway through, I remember my mother Elise's letter, which I've left under a sweater.

You could go home, Elise writes. *You could buy an apart-ment, begin to show things to people.* She's sent clippings from half a dozen art columns and magazines. Two are

by Schonberg, from whom I took a stained glass workshop long ago in New York.

A well-intentioned gesture, but a bad one. She doesn't
know what his name means to me.

I'm sorry that he had that horrible lapse in judgment, and I
hope you decided to travel for leaving's sake, and not because it
hurt too much not to. Expanding your horizons for their own
sake can be wonderful, but I would hate to think he has influ-
enced this precious time in your life. Remember those little peo-
ple and creatures you stuck in the back of the closet? she
continues in what I read as a non sequitur. *I took them*
to the boat and stuck candles on top. They're kind of lovely
that way. Maybe you'll come see.

I stop reading, annoyed not because she's lit on
something I know, but because what she says may be
true but has not occurred to me. Someone did show up
and tell me something important, which I had just begun to see in another way was my fault and his fault.
Next he backed up his point in a way that I will not be
able to forget easily. It's true that I decided to travel,
but does that mean that I am running toward myself or
away from him?

I wonder what Javier would think of all of that.

But I can't tell him. Not yet. I'm not properly tempered.

◊

I go out for a walk and find Javier's car parked up near
the studio. I peer through the windows at the little glass
creature locked inside. I'm looking for the angle that
will show me what he saw when he said he saw me in
it. I remember how when Elise was packing up after
she sold the house, she found a little girl-creature I'd
made in my first glass workshop. It had one glass hair
curled in a flip and knees pulled up to a chin five times

as wide as they were, and I wanted both to defend and banish it. Javier's horse has that same accidental eloquence. Yet while I stashed mine in a closet, he doesn't think twice about displaying his.

I'm still looking at it when Javier himself turns the corner. There is nothing to do but stand and wait for him. He looks pleased to see me: not less or more pleased than usual. Already, the beard is growing back in.

It's been a week since that early morning in Javier's apartment. I wonder if that's too much time, or too little. At least I know now why I left there during the rain. It wasn't to avoid more temper, or desire. It's the same reason we never make plans. If I stay once I'll need to show up regularly to prove to both of us that life is reliable. Once I begin, I can't end. I can't allow him the satisfaction of proving his point.

"How did you happen to be here?" he asks.

"I walk on Sundays. A lot. Would you mind driving me up to *telefónicas?*" I'm relieved he doesn't mention that morning, and that makes me braver bringing up a sudden desire I have. "I want to try to get my mother on the phone, and *telefónicas* closes in fifteen minutes."

The usually long Sunday line to make an overseas telephone call has thinned out; the woman at the desk motions me to one of the three phone booths almost immediately.

I don't know exactly what it is I'm going to say to Elise, but inside I feel the energy gathering. I want to find out what my words will be. The need feels almost physical.

Her assistant answers. Elise isn't home. She's out on a trip.

"Of course," I say. It's Sunday. Midseason. I should

have known. No, she can't call back, I'll have to write, I don't have a phone.

"Have her call you at my place in town," Javier says when I come out. He's watching me carefully. It's a look of concern.

"Nah, I don't know when she'll be back, it's too complicated to make an appointment." I hide my hands, which are shaking. Outside, the sky looks particularly bright. It's vibrating. I don't want to be under it.

"Want to go have lunch?" Javier says.

At one of the highway places he favors out of sight of the sea he urges meat, potatoes, sangria, and ice cream upon me.

"I don't eat like this," I protest.

"Real food," he opines.

"I have plenty of money, if that's what you're thinking. I don't live off the glass stuff, I have what is known as a little income. Okay?" But the food is settling me down again. Outside, the sky returns to its usual color. We joke awhile about people we both know and tell stories about goings-on in some of the more colorful bars in town.

"I'm getting angry again," he confides, almost to himself, as we push away from the table. "Sometimes I just get angry."

Again. That's interesting. It's the first reference he's made to the other morning.

"What about?"

The tone of voice he's used makes this temper sound like the sort of old friend you're bound to by history, not affection. This tone is calm: no melodrama. He sounds like me.

"We have this friend, Daniel," Javier offers. "He spent two years here building himself a sailboat. He just finished it. And now he went and got himself arrested for bringing in a little turd of hashish on the ferry from Tangier. He left the boat in Morocco. No one can understand it. Now the authorities have gone and impounded *Planetario,* his sailboat. Some of the gang want to buy it back for him, but I can't tell if it's that they want to do it for him, or for themselves. They are coming to my place, and I don't know what to say."

"I'll come with you," I say adding, "if you want."

"You will?"

"I will." I sound so sure of myself. I pause, looking at the horse. Something about the sweet little face he gave it strikes me as familiar. Something about it reminds me of the face of the girl in the photograph in his apartment. But Javier is glad I've suggested this. I have something to offer him, too.

"You're not going to get really angry again, are you?"

I've intended this as a joke, but the way he clenches his hands around the steering wheel as he slides behind it tells me that it's not a joke to him.

Neither of us says another word all the way to his place.

◊

Javier's tiny apartment is already filled with the sunset crowd and plates of food. The TV is on in the background. A girl from the restaurant finishes laying out cheese; she quietly leaves.

As we sit down, all eyes turn to Javier like plants to the sun. I feel their intensity pushing me out of the room. It's like volume displacement. None of these eyes settles on me, but it's not because I'm invisible. It's because I'm too visible, too big. I'm another plant, a closer one, who might block the light they need.

I sit down slightly behind Javier and listen as each

man pleads his case for the boat with a man who hates the sea. Javier, silent, looks from face to face as they speak. All his energy seems focused on protecting himself, on giving them nothing.

Javier starts to fiddle with a little tape player on the table until the sounds of guitars come out. As he does this, his face softens a little, and I feel better too. He's been remote since the moment in the car when I teased him about his temper, now I feel like that music is a message for me. I'm back in the room.

On the TV someone is interviewing a British soldier on a destroyer which is cruising toward the Falkland Islands.

"Do you like the Navy?" asks a voice off-camera.

"Yes sir," the soldier replies, so promptly that everyone in the room laughs.

Luis, a well-dressed kid of about twenty, reaches over and turns the sound down.

The guitar music ends. We hear the last scratches of the tape against the machine and an abrupt click reveals the room's intense silence. Abruptly, Javier rises to his feet.

I don't know if it's been the television or the music, or something about the conversation that's made him react this way, but the men know what it is. They all look down. A shadow crosses their faces as if they have been distracted by something far away. Their eyes lift to Javier's, which have gone bright and hard. They are clearly afraid of him. As if by silent agreement, every man rises and begins to help himself to more food.

"Tess," says Javier. "Let's get out of here." He tosses a key ring to the kid named Luis and we're gone.

◇

"They look like they think I'm going to give you the boat," Javier exclaims as we drive down the hill. "That's why I had to leave. People taking what isn't theirs. That's what makes me so angry. The boat is Danny's."

"I didn't know it was yours to give anyone. I thought it was impounded." I'm perturbed by this assumption he could get the boat back. What it might say about who Javier is, and how his sweetheart died, smacks of those names I don't like to hear people called. But then I think of what the letters I still receive from America say about me.

I file this all away for later. It's more interesting to recall the envy of those men's shoulders turning away as I walked into the room with Javier. I haven't been part of many groups in my life, I've almost always found myself one on one, or one on glass. I've withstood the envy of one. But being envied by a whole group is something new. It feels like a wave, instead of a whirlpool. It crests, shatters, and is gone. Whereas, experienced one on one envy feels huge, infinite.

"The boat's impounded." Javier sounds like he's far away. I decide to say no more. But he continues. "What's going on is, I have sway with people. So they think I can get them what they want."

"Can you?"

Javier's face saddens. "Where's my passport?" he asks suddenly, looking for his legitimate-issue, red-stamped REFUGIADO, which he usually places within arm's reach on the dashboard, next to the registration papers right before we go for a drive. He feels in all his pockets, then lifts up slightly to press the seat under him. "If the police pull me over again I'll probably get thrown out of the country." He swears quietly. "I could have sworn I had it when we went to the apartment," he continues.

"Could you have left it there?" I try to keep the tone of my voice level. Javier's the calm one. I've never seen him nervous. It's out of character.

"No." He scowls. "No."

We drive on silently for a moment. The car picks up speed.

"Whoa, Javier," I say. "If you're worried about the police, we should slow down."

For a moment he does, then speeds up again. Javier appears to be thinking rapidly, but all he says is, "Do you see those papers anywhere?"

I look at the backseat, the floor, my seat. The glove compartment is locked.

"You don't think someone took it, do you?"

"Goddamned terrorist passport." Javier turns onto an unfamiliar road. First I'm confused, then I remember there is a long way back to the middle of town along the water that starts like this. Javier reaches past me, unlocks the glove compartment, and gropes around inside. Out come a snapshot of a formal house on a bluish hill, some empty envelopes with Argentine postmarks, and a road map. Next he runs his hand along the crack behind the dashboard, comes up with a manila envelope, and hands it to me.

"Check here."

I put the envelope in my lap. The papers that fall out are flimsy and covered with scrawl. They look several years old. A photograph has fallen out, too, backside up. On front is the same face I saw on the wall of his apartment. This must be the girl he was talking about. *Soon,* the inscription says in Spanish. *Love, Maite.*

Javier glances in my direction. He makes a face.

"You can put the envelope down now."

We coast through the yellow flatlands behind town. The air is sweet with jasmine and exhaust and the roadside tables are filled with men and women playing cards in the sun. I realize that we passed our turnoff while I was looking in the envelope.

"Let's go find some beer," he suggests now. He turns once more, this time onto an older road that runs straight inland.

"There's beer back at your place." I speak carefully. "Food, too." We're heading into the middle of nowhere. There's no beer here.

Tree branches snap off against the car. Pebbles crackle and rub under the tires and bounce against the chassis. The sky is clear, but darkening, and there is no longer any sign that we are near the ocean at all. Time passes. I consider mentioning we've been on the road awhile, then decide against it. A lot of people drive to get calm again. A jackrabbit on the next rise sits up on his heels and darts off through the creosote. I follow its path for as long as I can until it stops looking like an animal and becomes just a disturbance in the field. Finally, I lose sight of it entirely.

Javier's face relaxes and I relax, too: his mood's passed. I begin to enjoy the scenery. I'm not nervous any longer about being so far from town.

Javier pulls off to the side of the road. He clenches and releases each fist.

"I think I'll get out for a minute." He opens the door on the driver's side.

I look at the land. I decide I'll stay where I am and try to find another rabbit.

Javier leaves the door open.

"I'm going to take a walk," he says loudly.

I nod. I'd feel better if there were more than two of us, if we were a group. Then whatever Javier is feeling might just crash over me and be gone, a wave. Instead, there are only the two of us and the alarm I felt has returned, it's a Möbius strip, it's infinite. I think, *Don't leave me.*

"Crazy." He points to his head. "I'm going to think a little."

I nod again. He points to his head, turns around, and begins to move through the brush.

I look at the sky and the leaves rising and falling softly with the breeze. I can see bees dipping into the bright and ragged cups of the summer flowers. Dust rises into the car.

When I shut his door the sound rings out over the valley.

Outside, Javier sits on a rock and holds his head in his hands.

I close my eyes, lean my head against the car door, and wait.

He sits there a moment, then looks one last time through his pockets for the passport. He taps his hand against his knee and gazes back along the road we've come on.

"Tess. Listen to me. This is bad. Take the car and go home."

I straighten in the seat. He's still sitting on the rock, but now he's looking at me, pleading.

"What's bad? What are you talking about, go home?"

"Listen to me. I made a mistake. This is important. Go home, and I'll come by when I can."

I feel that he's hit me.

"What are you going to do out here in the middle of nowhere by yourself?"

He speaks again, patiently. "I told you I like to spend time away from people. There is a map in the glove compartment. You saw." His manner reminds me of the pained courteousness he assumed the day I took him to the studio and we passed the shopgirls on the street. He is twenty feet away on a rock, but he makes this unusual request as if he's asking me to pass the salt.

"Does this have anything to do with those people at your place?"

"I am going to sit here until you leave."

For a while we just look at each other. I'm pretty good staring people down, but his eyes flare and his face darkens in ways that make looking at him hard. I pick up the little creature on the dashboard and turn it around and around in my hand.

Then it comes to me. This man is the shadow with eyes. I stare harder. I sit back and close my own eyes.

When I open them again he's gone.

CHAPTER THREE

◇

The land around me darkens and brightens in the shifting sun of late afternoon as I wait for Javier to come
back to me.

It's not so bad to be in the night. A sliver moon is
setting in the south and the sky is jittery with pale stars.
The complex scent of rich mud, dust, and grasses
washes over me as I walk up and down the road. In the
ditches, crickets are purring. My ear, ordering the sound
into something familiar, begins to hear guitars. It adds
the faintest chorus of male voices, it's the echo of something familiar: the melody of one of the songs on Javier's tape player. It gets a little louder. I'm not
imagining it.

I survey the fields on both sides of me. The human
music clings to the hills and trickles through the wind,
it's spread so thinly over the fields and through the air

that its location is as hard to determine as that of the crickets. Only the slow three-quarter time is unmistakable, and it codifies the sounds of the night for me the way a village church chime, no matter how unexpected, seems to order the cacophony of a village around it for a few brief seconds. The longer I look, the clearer things become. I see trees, then shrubs, then smooth brown boulders.

I find a stain of light on the northeastern horizon, across the field where I last saw Javier. More yellow than moonlight and facing out into darkness, it casts a faint elliptical shape down a slope and through a stand of thin trees. I close my eyes and try to locate the music, I try so hard to find its source my temples begin to pound and my eyes fill with tears. First it seems to come from the direction of the light, next it bounces away to a point behind me; then I am sure it is pouring down from the hills. But it always seems to go back to that light.

I think that's where the music's coming from.

I pocket the car keys and set off through the field.

PART II

THE WINDOW LOVERS

CHAPTER FOUR

◇

Slender orange trees fringe the crest of the hill.

I stand among them and look out at a crumbling terrace. It's lit by a carefully banked fire. Luis, the almond-
eyed blondish kid from Javier's apartment, and two
other men sit on the patio playing cards. The fire that
lies between us snaps sparks out onto the earth.

I want to speak to them, but I don't know how to
begin. So instead I hover just beyond the light cast by
the flames.

Immaculately groomed and aloof, Luis looks incon-
gruous sandwiched between the older, gruffer, darker
pair. I decide Luis is probably about my age.

The men are playing a languid game of poker. I look
at the assortment of beer bottles and glasses screwed
into the earth at their feet and decide it's been going on

for quite a while. It looks like a game being played to fill up time.

Behind, a long, lashed awning stretches out from a crumbling white stucco building. In the indistinct space darkness makes the building seem to stretch almost as far as the eye can see. Square lines and rows of small, shuttered darkened windows suggest an institution. But the remnants of a blue and gold tile frieze under the eaves and a dry tile fountain at one corner say something else.

"If Danny's luck hadn't run out on him we could have been—" one of the unknown men is speaking.

"Don't start," says the other, who is the larger and sturdier of the two. Both speak in Argentine Spanish.

"Will you pass me just a little water please, Eduardo?" asks Luis.

The man he has spoken to, who has curly salt-and-pepper hair, puts down his cards, rises to his feet, and walks back and forth from one end of the awning to the other.

"It's a goddamn shame," Eduardo says defensively. "A guy like that who was a friend to everyone." He kicks the ground. "Damn cornball music. Doesn't the boss keep anything else around?"

"Ho boy, easy now," says the larger man quietly.

"Tito's got something," says Luis.

"What, what's Tito got? Tito what you got?"

Eduardo struts close to the card table.

The big man, Tito, who has reddish hands and face and coarse black hair, puts down his cards and sighs quietly.

"People never really knew what was going on with Danny. I'm really sorry, 'uardo, and I feel great affection and sympathy for him right now. But the man has

tremendous resources of all kinds. In here," Tito points
to his own head, "and out here." He taps the pile of
coins and bills on the table. "The man is a juggler, a
very good juggler for a beginner."

"Nothing wrong with that," Luis says.

"Nothing at all," Tito agrees. "And with such a
tranquil disposition. He's still young. He'll grow and
survive."

Luis nods and slumps down in his chair.

"I must tell you, I'm afraid Danny is sometimes over-
confident, even though he doesn't seem to be," Tito
continues.

"Daniel is a poor slob like you and me who dreamed
of traveling around the world in his own home. He had
pathetic little dreams for his sainted little life and for-
tunately or unfortunately, he was just stupid enough to
try and carry them out. Period." Eduardo hits the table
with the back of his hand.

Tito and Luis exchange a look and Eduardo sits down
with them again. Tito picks up his hand and Eduardo
follows suit. Listlessly, they play through a hand.

"Fire's running low," Luis says then.

"Dawn approaches," Tito speaks dryly. "Dawn approaches."

"Let's hope Javier approaches along with those little
rosy fingers," says Eduardo.

"The boss is reliable," says Luis.

Dawn is bleaching the poplar trees and the poker
game in the clearing is breaking up. Luis gathers the
whiskey glasses in the crook of one arm as Eduardo
and Tito fold up the table and lean it against the wall.
Luis disappears inside with the glasses while Tito settles
back onto one of the folding chairs. Now Eduardo spits
on the ground, leans over, and turns over the tape in

the cassette player, which lies on the ground. Tito
shakes his shoulders in annoyance but says nothing.

> *yo quisiera vivir siempre a tu orilla,*
> *yo quisiera una choza guarnecida*
> *de agreste enredadera y sombreada . . .*
> *Al umbral de mi puerta una baraquilla . . .*

I listen: "I wish I could always live on your bank, in
a little cottage trimmed with shading vines, A little boat
moored just outside my door . . ."

Eduardo shakes his head back and forth. "Ain't it the
truth," he said. "It's the truth."

"Don't you get tired of it, man?" Tito asks mildly.

"It says something to me," Eduardo snaps. "It gets
into my soul."

"The truth is you can't stand silence for more than
two minutes." Luis has come outside again. "It makes
you nervous."

"Nervous? I'm just full of life," Eduardo says. "I'm
living high."

"I feel like some sleep." Tito pulls another folding
chair in front of him and stretches his legs out on it.

Luis sits down against the back wall of the building,
and lights a cigarette.

> *Río, que cruzas lentamente el llano,*
> *fecundando la tierra y dando vida*
> *a tristes sauces y álamos crecidos . . .*

Tito leans his head back and closes his eyes. "River," he slowly mouths along, "slowly you cross the
plain . . ." He stops. Soon his mouth drops open and

his breathing goes long. Luis stubs out the cigarette and closes his own eyes.

Eduardo paces back and forth until the song ends, stopping to pose and tap his foot now and then.

Then he walks around the left side of the building.

I follow him with my eyes, toward the ghostly green boat prow that is cleaving the mist just above the earth there, suspended in the cold lilac air of dawn.

I lie down in the earth and sleep.

CHAPTER FIVE

◇

I wake to the sound of someone laughing. It's a male laugh, a belly laugh that winds down and then widens out again. Someone is pulling me to my feet. Leaves stick to my clothes and to my hair. My mouth tastes like dirt. I open my eyes.

Javier is taking off his jacket and then he's wiping my face with it.

"Tessa, Tess. I told you to go home."

I can't think. I'm cold and stiff. Javier continues to dust me carefully.

"Look at yourself. Brambles!" He sighs, then chuckles. His face, though, is sad. It feels like mid-morning.

"You left me," I say, remembering.

"Gringa, gringa." His voice is sorrowful.

The space behind him is empty. Even the chairs and

bookshelves are gone. Clouds have swept in while I slept, and it feels like rain.

I turn my head sharply to the left.

I have not dreamed the boat.

It's scaffolded above the ground and the curved hull is silhouetted against the whirling gray sky. In some places, the hull is nothing more than its frame; elsewhere smooth planks finish the shape. Nearby, a drill and a toolbox lie on the ground.

"Luis went into town and left those tools there," Javier says, following my gaze. "He's the one who found you anyway. He came out here to take a leak. You sure scared him. He came and got me."

We face each other. We are both balanced slightly forward on the balls of our feet, hands thrust in our pockets. This is not the scowling face from the car, or the remote one that told me to go home. It is not even the face I knew in town: this is a face that moves.

"I'm sorry I left you," he says finally. "I'm sorry about that. But I never would have predicted you would show up here." He pauses. His face dances with thought. Abruptly, that turns to worry. "You know, this is a terrible idea."

"What is?"

He leans over, picks some crushed leaves out of my hair, and drops them to the ground. Several more emotions cross his face but I can't identify any of them.

"Come inside and get yourself cleaned up."

To my surprise, he leads me past the white house and around its side. I see the building is not as large as I thought: it's more an estate than an institution. Several small wings that seem to have been added at different times are what give it that odd shape and faint air of communal complexity. Azaleas soften the edges and knit all the parts into a whole. Although the windows retain most of what had once been fancy iron grillwork, much of the glass is broken. I take in the curved pieces of glass still stuck in the frames. They have the random undulations and streaks of the old hand-rolled panes. The chipped and faded multicolored tile mosaics I glimpsed during the night border the entire roof. Tiled murals along the walls interpret the Dance of the Hours in a turn-of-the-century style.

Javier notices me noticing the mural.

"Got to have that restored," he says.

I turn around. Behind us and past the house the hill falls off and I can see the terrain of my nocturnal journey spread out before me. The greenish-gray fields flecked with coppery shrubs pour on in large and gentle waves to the road.

The white car is gone.

I finger the keys in my pocket.

When I start walking again, Javier leads me around the front of the house to a long field, and next to that, a gleaming aluminum trailer. He keeps stealing little glances at me. Each time he does this I feel more bashful. I'm full of unseemly awareness of him.

As he guides me around the house and toward the trailer, his steps lighten. He watches me take in the house, the trailer, and the little camp stove standing in front of the trailer.

"Do you like my new property?" he asks finally, beginning to reheat coffee on the stove. It's a sincere question and it disarms me a little.

"I don't know what it is, but it looks like it used to be a special place."

"It was. It is. It used to be a retreat for rich señoras, before the *guerra civil*. A sanitarium."

"And now what is it?"

"Call it a refuge. For everyone. For you."

"Even me."

"You're welcome here. It's true I wish you weren't here, but now that you are . . ."

"What's going on here?" I speak reluctantly, and I speak for both of us. He looks relieved, even approving. It's like I've passed a test.

"I'm getting involved in politics again," he says, almost bashfully. "You know. I need a safe place."

"Well. I'm happy for you, I guess."

"Soon I'll be going home."

From where we are standing the boat looks like it's sailing across the top of a poplar grove.

"You think I have something you want," he concludes.

"What's going on here?" I repeat. "No, I don't want to know."

"You're not usually so contradictory." He sounds gleeful.

I want to be angry with him, but I can't manage it. I want to know what's going on here and I don't. But I feel so at home with this man that this feeling of comfort overrides all others. That saltwater substance inside me is being matched by something in him. *Hippi, mafioso, ladrón.* I know those words can also be applied to me. As we walk, a delicate negotiation is taking place between Javier's larger purpose and this business of living day by day. As long as the balance holds, everything will be ordinary. If I disrupt it, some extraordinary thing may be released.

Javier bends over the coffeepot. I notice a new intensity and fastidiousness to his gestures.

I need to be alone. Alone as I can be. Javier's back is

still turned as I walk up the traces of what was once a gravel path to the wide, dark veranda of Los Ane-nomes, which is what a small card stuck on the front door glass proclaims it to be. I close my eyes and feel my body pound. Soon I hear his step behind me.

He sits down next to me and puts a mug of coffee on the floor.

"Isn't it *anemone*?"

"Yes," he replies. "Someone misspelled it. But I like it that way. A kind of joke."

"What's inside?"

"Stock. Overflow from the bar."

"Is that what Luis was drinking last night while he was waiting for you?"

"Was he?" Javier chuckles. "Luis is my cousin, you know."

We drink our coffee.

"I didn't think you'd follow me! Any other *chabala* would have gone home!"

"I don't know how to drive a stick shift," I lie.

He stops laughing, narrows his eyes, and stands up. He walks to the edge of the veranda, looks out, and turns around. He looks faintly disappointed about something.

"I waited in your damned car forever. Finally I saw a light and followed it here."

"You didn't have to come this way. There's a turnoff for this place just a few kilometers from where I left the car. Next time, feel free to use the front door."

"Did you ever stop to think I'd worry about you? Or, that I might not know how to drive at all?" My head feels tight. I wish I'd never come here. "It would be easier to know how to act if your life wasn't so damn strange."

"Strange, what's strange? This is how life is. It's always like this, deep down. I knew you can drive. It came up once," he adds as an afterthought.

Javier looks me up and down. I look back. He's wearing a fresh blue shirt and his hair is shower-damp. His eyes have a light and focus that is new. He's all quiet focus, waiting. I feel completely exposed and fully alert. I sense every cell in my body, every inch of rough surface on the wood veranda; the sun, the air, the pulse beating in each bird and the sap rising in each tree as its branches shake and the bird flies away.

"I don't know the first thing about you," I say.

"You know everything about me."

Right then I become sure of something, sure enough to try it out. Being sure makes me feel subdued but clear, like when things look better and calmer after a long cry.

I move toward Javier until we are face to face. As I approach, his focus retreats and when I'm next to him I feel him go very still.

"Now," I say, and he places his hands on my shoulders. He receives me.

Softly, barely breathing, I reach out blind and run my forehead across his lips.

What I want to do has been as hidden as light by a wall of rock. But even so, once you make one little chink in such a wall, light is suddenly and unequivocably there.

Javier sighs, and starts to ask me something. Then he stops, brushing the cup away, takes hold of my hair and turns my head toward his. It's been a long time since I've been with a man, and now I want him just as hard as I wanted the light on the hill, and with just as little idea of what he might hold for me as I'd had of it. We take each other slowly while the poplar branches click and slither above us and tiny animals skitter over the walls.

But as we slip deeper and deeper and he groans a little and swears and clutches handfuls of me with his small, exact, iron fists, as he becomes someone new, I remember his unspoken dare: stay with me, stay alive. These words run through my mind for a long time. *Stay with me, stay alive. Stay with me, stay alive. Stay.*

CHAPTER SIX

◇

I come to. I feel alert and calm. My strength is right there. That's good. Because before I started traveling, I'd been afraid I would never find it the way everyone else seemed to.

All I have to do now is remember once more, and forget forever. I can do it up here. It will be easy. What an odd little kinship there is between memory and desire. I'd forgotten. They can both be so hard to summon up, but then when you least expect it one sounds and the other chimes right in. That makes me understand why I've chosen to live the way I have for such a long time. I'm remembering.

I had gone to play in the circle of boulders at the edge of our woods that morning while Elise and my stepfa-

ther, Lars, moved my stepbrothers Adam and John into
their room. The boulders were yellow, and the size of
large animals. Huge chips of rock had been hewn out
of their sides, leaving behind hemispheres and deep
wedges of space big enough for me to sit in or use as
steps to pull myself up on top. Bob, my father, had told
me the Ice Age had carried the boulders down from the
North and abandoned them where they stood. But I
found it difficult to believe such a random and furious
force could have abandoned this collection in our yard
without leaving any at all for the neighbors. A more
ominous possibility had occurred to me: that the neighbors had also found boulders in their yards, but had
removed them for pressing reasons my parents fool-
ishly had ignored.

By then, Bob was not always present to disperse my
fears with his soothing explanation of the forces of na-
ture. He and Elise, my mother, relinquished the house
to each other every six months, retiring to the same
long-term rental in the center of town for the other six.
At ten I was dimly aware of the precariousness of such
an arrangement. But they were both careful not to let
the glum makeshiftness of their own lives intrude on
the placid appearance of life on the hill, at least not
for the first two cycles of the agreement, which had
been laboriously crafted by lawyers. But during the
third cycle Elise, who was in residence at the time, married Lars, and he and Adam and John moved in.

On that morning, the boys had appeared in the yard
followed by Elise and Lars. I had met them only twice
before, once at a museum and then again at the wedding. Adam, who was only six months older than I
was, was thin and milky-skinned. John, who was two
years younger, was chubby and ruddy. They were both
quite fair. Each boy had a brand-new Swiss Army knife

hooked to the belt loop of his jeans. Adam and John were from New York and knew nothing about the country or the woods.

I started to scratch patterns on my boulder with pebbles. I studied these patterns while Adam and John circled all my rocks, pressed their cheeks against them, and examined the tart crabgrass that grew at their bases even in February. But something deterred them from actually climbing on top. Stymied, they fell abruptly silent. I could hear my heart beating quickly and I felt Elise's eyes on me from the top of the yard. I could hear nothing but John's soft, slightly congested breathing. And then Adam trudged to the edge of my woods.

Over the fall and into the winter, during all the fuss surrounding the wedding, I had been spending a lot of time in the woods. I loved to walk through them after a snowfall, to leave crisp leafy footprints and hunt down the few wild flowers that still poked up. I had my favorite places: the boulders at the edge, the rock fence that seemed to slide out of the ground farther in, the stream at the heart, and the dump at the back boundary. In the spring and summer my friends came, but in the winter I went alone. At times I became extremely conscious of just how alone I was in there and how anything could happen. But the woods were still the place I felt most like myself.

Now Adam pushed his foot back and forth in the grass where the smallest trees started, as if he were clearing a path. Then he grabbed the trunk of a young birch, lifted his face, and shook. Bits of ice and dirt rained down. Stepping back, he approached John, who had been watching us both. They whispered together.

"Would you like to come into town?" Adam called in a clear, authoritative voice. "We're going into town."

I looked up. He blinked and looked at the ground. It

was odd to hear him say, "into town," as if it were his town. He had never even been there.

"Thanks," I said, "but I've got some things to do here."

"Draw on rocks?" he said.

"No," I said. "Other things."

During those late-winter months my stepbrothers and I forged an unspoken agreement: in the house and yard we would know each other, but from the boulders on through the woods we would remain strangers. Each time I watched their pale silhouettes disappear between the dogwoods I felt like someone had taken advantage of me. This feeling would be followed by a fury that surprised me into complete blankness, and I'd go into the woods myself to roam away this strange combination of feelings.

The boys and I crossed paths so often there I began to wonder if they were following me and perhaps even if their goal was to entice me into the forest. Soon we had a ritual: I'd head out toward one of my usual destinations, and about ten minutes into the brush I'd hear them, whispering and slinging pebbles to my right or left.

"Do you want to come?" I'd call then, and they'd shuffle up to my side murmuring to each other as if they were rejoining a tour group from which they'd briefly strayed. They always looked so harmless, so inept, so ignorant that I felt sorry for them and for my unkind feelings. Then together we would continue to my stream, or to the fence of flat rocks that looked like the scales on a brontosaurus spine. Briefly repentant, I would reason it was inevitable that they find my secret places, and that those places had never belonged to me

exclusively. It was true that once we'd dispensed with
the preliminary shadowing, my new stepbrothers became subdued and respectful. It looked as though they
were beginning to love the woods as I did, and the sight
of a certain bend in the stream where you could sit on
a slanted rock and watch a cache of translucent frogs'
eggs tremble and glint in the soft fall of a moss dam
was enough to quell any incipient mischief, at least for
the time being.

It was at the stream where they began to ask the puzzled, rhetorical questions about my mother: "She really
likes old-fashioned music, doesn't she?" or, "She really
gets mad in the morning if you wake her up." Hearing
Elise discussed by strange boys was in itself as startling
as the things they actually said about her, which pin-
pointed troubling attributes familiar to me too, but
which I considered as immutable as the boulders themselves and never would have considered objecting to. I
was mesmerized: when they praised her I felt proud,
then jealous of their access to her. When they were un-
flattering I would first defend her, then secretly agree
with them, and end up mortified. For my part I couldn't
even have begun to ask them about Lars.

Instead I showed them the Sky Tooth, the smooth
triangle of blue porcelain I always carried with me. I
told the boys the Sky Tooth had been left for me by
fairies who had retreated farther into the woods. The
Sky Tooth, I said, endowed its bearer with special pow-
ers of vision. The woods, I told them, looked different
to me, but I'd do my best to explain what they were
missing.

They eyed it sulkily.

In fact, I'd found the Sky Tooth at one of the few
places in the woods I wanted, for reasons I couldn't

explain, to keep from them. And one day in early spring, as we drove home from the grocery store, my mother betrayed it to them.

"Why, it's getting warm," she said. "The snow is all gone. Your old dump will be good for the getting."

The dump lay deep in the woods, a sudden, yellow, mealy-earthed clearing about as wide as a road and a few hundred feet long. Fragments of colored glass and shards of kitchen pottery poked out of the ground like scales or frozen waves. And while the trees near our house were slight or graceful, moist birches or leafy oaks crowded in a contest of growth, the trees near the dump became tall, spare, and brittle, and were populated with large, unfamiliar birds that flapped off when I approached. The dump was my boundary. The brush on the other side looked dense, the spaces between the trees narrow and foreboding. I had never been there.

"What is this place?" Adam whispered to me as we got out of the car.

"It's kind of creepy. I don't go there so often."

"Did you get that blue clay there?" he asked, meaning the Sky Tooth.

"Yes." I paused, shocked at my own admission. "I did."

"I want to go."

"It's not dry enough," I said, stalling. I couldn't say why I didn't want to take him there, but I knew it would be the start of something I wanted to avoid. "It's hard to find stuff in the mud."

"All right. You let me know, though. I bet I can find it anyway."

One week later, my mother came home to find Adam carving his name on her original cast recording of *Showboat* with his Swiss Army knife. She slapped him twice in front of me and pushed him upstairs to his room.

By midafternoon both boys were watching me carefully, as though I were a suspect they couldn't let escape. As I moved from room to room, one or the other moved with me. I escaped to the front yard and soon they were loitering under the crabapple tree.

"We'd really like to go to the dump today," Adam informed me. "We'd really appreciate it if you could take us away from here."

"Is the dump where you got the Sky Tooth?" John asked shyly. I nodded and he unhooked his own knife from his belt and held it out to me. "I'll give you this if we can go," he offered.

Adam turned away from us slightly.

"Keep it," I said. "Sooner or later you'd get there some other way."

And so we went.

As the trees grew large and black, a certain flush on Adam's cheeks and a hard shine in both boys' eyes confirmed that, as I had expected without knowing why, this particular conquest was especially exciting for them.

I uttered brief commands: "Be careful." "Stay back." "Don't fall behind." Of this last, there was no danger. Adam and John were right at my sides, and John, who was slightly asthmatic, was breathing heavily.

"Vulture," Adam spat softly, stopping to look at one of the elaborate dead trees. He made clicking noises.

"Sssss," whistled John, and all around us I could hear animals alerted, rising, moving away.

Finally I saw the abrupt patch of space instead of trees and we approached the yellow scar in the earth. We stopped at the edge, as we would have stopped at the edge of a narrow and turbulent river. Winter had loosened its surface, and I could see the newly exposed case of an old-fashioned radio. The base and springs of a familiar brown couch had been exposed down to a fringe of colorless tassels. But most remarkable, as always, were the bright fragments of glass and crockery scattered about like raw seed of domestic life by some simultaneously destructive and nurturing primordial hand.

"The Ice Age did that," I said offhandedly. "My father told me."

"They didn't have cups and saucers in the Ice Age," Adam said scornfully. "No way."

"No way," echoed John.

I climbed onto a rock that was just slightly smaller than my boulders. "Okay," I said, not feeling okay at all. "Soon it's going to get dark."

They exchanged glances. Adam pulled a roll of twine from his jacket, cut some off, pulled it tight, and held it up to the landscape.

"Couch probably has worms," he said.

He and John marked, surveyed, and excavated with the help of the twine and some sticks they sharpened with their knives. Then they brought their booty back to the rock, where I sorted it, piled it, and waited anxiously, unable either to join them or to abandon them.

Adam raised his head and froze. A rustling sound was coming from the woods beyond the landfill. The rustling grew louder, and a large, purple-brown bird shook itself free from the foliage and winged vigorously toward the sky. Dead branches clattered.

Adam turned to me.

"What's back in there?" he demanded.

I told him I didn't know.

"Liar," he said.

"Liar, liar, barn's on fire," added John.

"I haven't ever been any farther than this." My voice was firm.

A wedge of blackbirds flew slowly across the gap in the trees. They were cawing softly. It took a long time for the whole flock to pass, and as they passed the air began to show the first tinges of deep purple that signal the coming of night. The shadows were going purple, too, and the yellow earth seemed to lose some of its lividness. I began to feel uneasy.

Adam looked at me the way he'd looked at my mother that morning.

"I have special information," he said. "Information I can't give you. But the point is, if John doesn't get to a plant that grows only in that part of the woods, his asthma will get very bad and he might die." Adam gave John a quick warning look.

John's jaw dropped, his face reddened, and he began to cry.

"I'm sorry," Adam continued, "but Dad told me. It was supposed to be a secret unless there was an emergency."

"Lars told you what?"

"That if it happened, a certain plant that grows only there would help John. Dad told me especially."

I looked at John. His nose was running and he *was* beginning to breathe very heavily, although he'd seemed fine before. He looked from Adam to me and tears flowed down his cheeks.

"When was Lars ever back there?" I wanted to know.

"Don't you remember that Sunday?" Adam's voice was unnecessarily loud. "That Sunday him and your mom went for a walk?"

I did remember. It had been after brunch on a Sunday

when Lars put down the football (he'd been teaching us how to kick), told us he'd be right back, and gone into the house. He and Elise had come back out about fifteen minutes later and wandered slowly toward the woods, pointing out the different kinds of trees to each other.

"Dogwood," my mother had said, fingering one of the white buds.

Then Lars had added, "Pink *and* white." They both had seemed quite pleased to know all the names of the trees. When Lars didn't know the name of a tree Elise would, and vice-versa. In this fashion they had eventually disappeared down the path to the woods that started near the hammock.

"What about it?" I inquired now.

"That walk was to find the plant. Dad does that wherever we go. And then they told me."

John, by this time, was quite red, and heaving.

"Liar," he sputtered. "Dad never told me."

"It was my responsibility," Adam said calmly.

I looked from one to the other. It was hard to tell what was true. Then I remembered the uncomfortable, lit-from-within look Elise's face had held the day the boys came to live with us. Why couldn't we just take all the new parts of life in stride without drawing too much attention to what was unusual? her face had seemed to say. It was like learning a new dance step, she seemed to imply. To catch on, you just had to try. So with her face before me I experienced the relief of believing him and asked Adam, "How do you know what the plant looks like?"

"Dad showed me a picture," he explained.

"We have to hurry," I said. "I'm not sure I can get us back if it gets dark."

The earth felt spongy where I stepped. I thought of all the layers and layers under my feet, the simple things buried there which had so soothed lives they were never broken or misplaced but were finally laid to rest. I couldn't understand why people did that, but it made me feel sad. I felt like I was stepping on some sort of grave. I never wanted to understand this kind of sadness.

The ground on the far side of the dump was covered with dead leaves, and the long shadows made the brush look even more dense than it really was. I couldn't see much between the trees but some brown vines.

"Is that it?" My voice was sharp.

"No." Adam seemed very calm, but Lars got that way too, especially when he was explaining something someone had done wrong, and why.

A shelf of very pale moss grew across one side of a dead stump. Ants crawled between the layers of rotting wood.

"What about that?"

"I'll tell you when." But he and John were falling behind. "When Dad finds out you let my brother die," Adam called, "he'll kill you."

It was hot in front of my face, and tiny bugs were buzzing all around me. My feet kept moving automatically, and my elbows and shins were latticed with tiny bleeding scratches.

In a low drift of dead leaves, I saw an unusual white flower. It was a long, fluted tube at the end of a thick green stem with a single sharp, arching leaf to either side. I leaned down to it. It had no smell.

"It's here! It's here!" I shouted.

But when I turned around there was no one.

I stood there and an ache started in my chest that

grew and grew until it was bigger than I was and was slicing the trees and I had to run. I heard more running behind me. I stopped and looked but I couldn't see anyone, although I thought I heard coughing and whispering. I ran, and stopped again, again, maybe three more times. Night pulsed down, staining the air.

A pale shining globe burst out of the line of trees in front of me. It was the top of John's head, and he was running, his shoulders pushed forward, his head pressed down like a bull's. As he careened into me I fell against his brother's shoulders. I was conscious of them pushing and pulling me and then I was backed up against a tree and Adam was tying my hands behind it with his twine. I could hear his quick breathing. He made a slow and careful knot.

"What *is* this?" I shouted. "Come *off* it!"

"Tighter," John said in his most authoritative voice.

"No," said Adam, almost gently. "We don't want to cut her wrists."

I tried to pull free, and John's small, damp, chubby hands closed around mine. Meanwhile, Adam stuck his hand between the twine and my wrists, testing and measuring until he was satisfied.

"Stay there," he said to John, and came around the front of the tree.

I spat at him. Tears burned my face.

He looked me in the eye. I kicked air.

"Do it," Adam said to John.

Adam's hands left my hands, reached around my waist, and tore my pants and underpants down to my ankles. Air rushed around me as though someone were dangling me off a cliff.

"I'm telling Mom," I screamed.

The pink circles on Adam's cheeks deepened. He

froze, his knees slightly bent as if he were skiing, his head tilted, his mouth slightly open as though he had something to say but had thought better of it.

Bark was raking my bare hips. I bent and twisted, but it only made me more aware of my nakedness. I began to tremble with the knowledge that all the creatures of the forest were sizing me up for their own bestial purposes.

Adam came close and rested one cold hand right above my pubic bone. With intense concentration, he looked at the place his hand was, and moved his gaze down to where it wouldn't go. Something like a shadow crossed his brow. Slowly, slowly, he lifted the hand, drew it back, and put it carefully inside his jacket pocket.

"Okay," he said.

John jerked my shirt and jacket up to my neck. Adam laid his open palms flat across my flat chest. I looked away. Quickly, he stooped and plucked the Sky Tooth from my front pants pocket, where it lay half exposed, and backed off slowly.

John loosened the twine binding my hands and suddenly they were gone, two pale and quickly moving suns swallowed up by dusky crevasses of the forest.

Then I was walking quickly in the opposite direction. I couldn't quite get my balance and more than once I grazed a tree with a wrist or shin and watched the white lines pop up on my skin. I could see the white lines even though the trees and wells of space in the far and middle distances were almost black. Then the forest noise flattened out and the blackness began to open. Far away, a red car whipped by. I ran inside the smooth borders of the gray-purple road, listening to my footsteps and calming myself. I ran for a long while, and

by the time I turned onto our street I had walked away
the deep white scrape of humiliation to encounter
something else, something wiser that I couldn't name,
in its place.

Yellow light was spilling out of our house. An ex-
pansive, breezy, surprising hum that tickled my ribs like
a steady wind floated me across the lawn and into the
dining room, where Elise was serving a tuna casserole.
As I took my place at the table, the boys' faces swiveled
toward the sinuous movement of the silver serving
spoons in her hands and she smiled a mistaken smile of
maternal triumph. Then she looked at me as if we two
were all alone, saying, "Now isn't their color high?"

And it was then, as I gazed upon those stricken faces,
that I knew the name for this interesting way I was
feeling. So this was what power felt like: all this pain
and peace and possibility wrapped up in one sturdy
parcel.

"Nah," I said, "that's just from playing ball down
the circle."

The pair of shocked faces blurred with relief. Grate-
fully, I surrendered to the ordinariness of dinner.

"We didn't mean anything," Adam said later.

I looked up at him carefully and briefly, as if he were
a light that hurt my eyes. Then I turned back to the
flowers I was pressing. Inspired by the warm evening,
Elise and I had gone out with flashlights for cuttings
from the dogwoods, which were finally in full bloom.

"Can we go back and get the stuff we got at the
dump?" he said very quickly.

I knew I could be both soft and strong with him, just
as I had known to take only a few dogwood blossoms
and leave the rest.

"Once it's out, it's out," I said. "And you know the

way. But go by the road. The rest's off limits until you have permission. Do you promise?"

"Okay," he said casually, and I knew his word was good.

The light at Los Anenomes is dark and oaky for noon. Suddenly I want to be out in the sun, but getting there is like jumping into an ice-cold pool. Javier raises himself up on one elbow. His face is introspective, remote, and I'm drawn again. Even though he seems far away, there is a vulnerability to his distance I haven't seen up close since I left my own country.

The light changes again and Javier hides his face in one hand. When the hand comes away his eyes roll up and down my body and I know him well enough to know he's appraising me in a manner not unlike the one he uses to appraise his horses. Coming from him, it's a compliment.

I wonder how it is that I can be so passionate and so detached at the same time.

"Fetch a good price?" I ask when he's done.

He snorts and reaches for his coffee cup. It's odd how that stillness is no longer the first thing I notice about him, how it's receded behind inflections and moods as subtle yet influential as a change in light.

"Good enough," he says. "You'll do."

We walk into the trailer and out of the noonday sun.

"My other house," says Javier. If we look at each other, our eyes get a soft inward focus and we're both the sort who feel lost without a sharp edge. So we take care to keep our eyes on other things yet still stand

close enough to perpetuate the soft current that together we make.

The trailer is furnished in royal blue and smells new.
A stack of papers and ledgers lie on the kitchen table,
but except for a little bathroom, well stocked with new
French-made towels and soap, the place seems empty.

"I'll make coffee," promises the man who makes
nothing but mate. Then he squeezes me on the rump
and leaves.

The dribble that comes out of the showerhead is just
warm. I try to see my apartment and the glass studio.
Blue vase, yellow flowers, two ripe peaches. Punty, pli-
ers, crucible. In my mind's eye, I lay out my tools on
the workbench and say the name of each.

But I can still feel the long, low walk I took through
the night, and the way Javier held me as if I were an
elixir saving him. Everything else seems wan and trivial
in comparison.

I used to wonder what Javier, who hated water, saw
in the sunset crew and their sailing dreams. But now I
see easily. Their sloop is just like his lost estate, the
house with rooms enough for everyone on endless,
empty fields. Their sloop is Los Anenomes.

I remember how the men have to be out there, in the
water, in the middle of nowhere before they can begin
to talk about what happened before.

Daniel. It's not a name I've ever heard at sunset. Now
I wonder why. I still can't see what Javier means when
he says he is getting back into politics. I add an impounded sailboat and a forgotten house to everything I
know or have heard about him. Still nothing. I add the
face and the handwriting of the girl named Maite. I still
don't have all the fragments I need, I can't piece this
picture together.

The little window in the trailer's bathroom is made

of frosted louvers that crank open with a little metal handle, like the windows in city row houses. It's odd to spy out the cracks and see nothing but a slice of hill, or sky, or grass.

Glass is something I can piece together.

The day after I joined the glass studio here, the group had a date to build a new kiln. I pitched in. I had to. Even after the years away those bricks had snapped into place like pieces of a puzzle. When it was done I stood with the others. They looked over with satisfaction. I looked with alarm. There the kiln was in all its particularity: able to destroy and create; to hold things in or keep them out.

The years between seemed to vanish.

I had started when I was fifteen. I barely knew who I was, and it simply felt reassuring to be able to create so much something out of nothing. Blowing glass is the purest expression of will: I'd read that somewhere and it still makes sense to me. A finished piece is a record of a form you will with your breath.

After those first experiments I put aside blown glass and went in other directions: less heat, less weight; more light and pattern. I tried stained glass, fused glass. And I began to work big. And I felt lucky to have stumbled onto a medium that held an inner dimension. I knew I was taking something very special I had inside and giving it a shape and form others could see. It had movement, and it had stillness.

It was at college, when that space inside was lost to me. I woke up one morning and looked at a piece I'd made: an etched black platter, hard and curved like obsidian. It was fascinating and slightly repellent, like the shell of a very beautiful insect. No longer "nothing" at all. Totally opaque. No inner dimension to speak of.

That's it, I thought. *It's over.* It was like acknowledg-

ing the death of a loved one. You become conscious of
time rearranging itself. What was infinite becomes
something finite to push off from. You can praise the
life, and you can judge it. Suddenly, the person who
has held you in thrall is gone.

Such a view is too intimate, the first shock of it vi-
olates both the one who is left and the one who is gone.

I saw the shape of a whole life when I saw that platter.

I'd thought I'd had a calling, and that what came of
that was one of the only things that was unequivocally
your own forever. *Talent is indestructible,* Elise used to
say. But the day I saw the platter clearly I understood
she had not told the entire truth. I saw him all over it.
I saw how he had marked me, and how I had marked
him.

And now I have not seen him for over a year.

CHAPTER SEVEN

◇

By the time Luis drives up in the white Fiat it's afternoon and once again Javier and I are drinking coffee from mugs on the side of the hill. I like how the handle and the sides of the metal cup almost scald my hands, jolting me into awareness.

Silently, Luis joins us on the little ridge. Javier leans back on his hands. He closes his eyes halfway, intent on some interior calculation.

He and I meet eyes and smile. Then we both look away.

"Tessa followed me here because she was worried about me," Javier says loudly. He digs his heel into the soft side of the hill.

Luis gazes down into the valley in response. As usual, he looks as if he's just combed his dark-blond locks and put on fresh clothes.

In Luis's silence Javier seems to darken and grow. His strength takes him over again; the moderating contentment I sometimes see fades and draws inside. I think of a thunderhead and a sun that share a single life force.

"Luis is genteel like you, Tessa. Me, I'm a boor. Life hasn't given me the opportunity to try my hand at anything else."

"Yes, that's true," I say slowly, adjusting to the new sound in his voice. So the thunderhead is impersonal, no one is exempted from the wake of its force. "And it never will, either, but saps like Luis and me will be fascinated by you anyway, and wonder why."

"I am also fascinated by what I need." Javier glances at me. "I look at pictures of my home, my ranch. I can't go back there. I am fascinated by its smallest window and the putrid little puddle where the kitchen plumbing runs off into the yard." He points his coffee cup at Los Anenomes. "I am even fascinated by this rotting carcass of an estate, and that is because I—"

Javier stops himself.

Luis blinks and wakens from his reverie. Sometimes he appears grief-stricken; at others, bored. He's always struck me as very loyal to Javier, but they are so different from each other it's hard to tell if Luis's loyalty comes from duty, self-interest, or nothing more than lack of any other purpose. It might be affection, but it isn't love.

"It doesn't sound right, *jefe*," he says softly now.

"It sounds like a lie?"

Luis turns back to look at the car. He notices I am also watching the white Fiat. He won't meet my gaze.

"I brought groceries and something to drink," Luis says. "And some fresh clothes for Tessa."

"Well then," says Javier.

All around us the world is quiet, save for the creaks the wooden boards of the veranda make as they shift in the wind. Up on the hill, part of the unfinished sailboat is covered with a tarp, and now the tarp begins to snap. A yellow pickup truck moves slowly down the road in the valley. It's the first vehicle I have seen travel that road aside from the white Fiat. The tarp begins tossing and turning.

"Che," Javier says to Luis. "See if we can't do something about that. If this cloth blows away the wood will warp."

Luis nods silently, shuts his eyes for a second, and sets off down the hill.

Javier lightens and relaxes visibly.

"He is not my cousin," Javier says when Luis is out of earshot. "We just call him that. He is the brother of the woman I was going to marry. He is the brother of Maite"

The yellow truck is on the verge of passing out of sight. It gets smaller and smaller, like the tiniest of flames at the edge of a burning log. Then it disappears.

"You are deciding whether you would like to be in that truck," Javier says after a pause.

"Yes, I am."

Javier runs the knuckles of his left hand up the inside of my thigh and rests his hand at the top.

"Please stay. Now that you're here."

"My guess is now that I am here I don't have a real choice."

"No. Not a real choice. For your own security. I would worry. Just a little. At the moment." He speaks so quietly these words ease into our conversation without so much as a ripple.

I finger the set of car keys in my pocket.

"I guess I'm not going to ask."

"Please don't." Now he's courteous, correct.

"Why did you drive me halfway out here?"

"I wasn't thinking exactly straight."

"You always think straight." I look off after the truck.

"Not always. You've seen that."

"So was I, what do they call it, your cover for something?"

"I got angry. I didn't know where I was going until I got here."

"But you did. And you stopped short of driving all the way here."

He shrugs. "I have no excuses. I didn't know I needed one. Once I found myself driving here I did not want to complicate matters for you."

What matters are you complicating? I wonder silently. Out loud I say, "You could have turned around and gone back."

He nods briefly, a salute to logic. "I could have."

"Find your passport?"

"No."

"Get that boat back?"

"No."

I don't respond.

"You're here." He speaks quietly. "What's done is done. I can't do anything about it." He pauses. And repeats, a little louder, "I can't do anything about it."

I can see Luis bending over the edge of the boat tarp, where the ropes were staked into the ground. The canvas keeps flapping away from him.

Javier takes me by the shoulders and turns me toward him. He looks incredibly sad. He runs his hands down my neck and shoulders and starts to unbutton my shirt.

"No, not a real choice," I say.

"No," he says. "No."

◇

Later, before Luis can rejoin us, I wander back to the trailer alone. I lie down on the couch. I stay there for a while, just looking up at the ceiling. Then I fall asleep.

"Vamos, Tess," says Javier. *"Ándale."*

He cradles and coaxes me until I'm sitting up. It's dark again. Luis stands behind Javier with his back turned.

"Where are we going?"

"To the house. We're going to sleep in the house. Luis is staying here."

Suddenly I am wide awake and we are walking down the hill. I look back and see a lantern in the trailer window, and Luis's shadow rocking back and forth, back and forth.

The building is pitch black. Javier shows me where to step. Over this board. Watch for that corner.

He stops in a room where something soft and substantial like dry, warm, whispering snow clings to our feet. I can tell by the white shape at the end of the black that there are some rolled-up blankets on the floor. Javier sits down and holds out his hands to me. I take them, and he pulls me down and extinguishes any feeling of separation I may have had in his arms. I still can't see much, but now I can feel him.

"We can't have any candles," he explains in a clear voice. "There is too much dry wood here."

For a while we touch each other, hard, as if neither of us knew the other one was there. Then Javier cups my hands with his own. Next he scoops the dry snow up off the floor and lets it fall into the hole my hands make. The dry snow is sawdust. He pulls my hands toward his body and separates them so that the sawdust falls on his chest. Then he pulls my hands back to the floor and we repeat the ritual.

"Do you understand?" he says.

"No."

He pulls my head toward him until my ear is next to his mouth.

"Bury me."

I can hear him breathing quietly as I rain sawdust over him. Each time I stop he asks me to go on.

He twitches as I cup the shavings around him. What I'm doing makes me wonder about the story he'd told me about his girlfriend that morning in his apartment, the one who may be called Maite. But it isn't a bad feeling. Soon my eyes adjust to the blackness and I find deep piles of the sawdust in corners formed by the stacked crates that fill the room. These piles are damp and coarse enough for me to move them in armloads, like fallen autumn leaves, and pack them around his chest and shoulders and legs.

Right now, I am not sure if I am being an active or reactive person.

When he is buried up to the neck, I run my hands over the surface of the dust for a while, as if I am passing a lazy hour at the beach.

Then I print his soft grave with my body, pressing down through the shavings until I feel his skin on my skin. Then, slowly, we both push away the sawdust and he holds my wrists so hard it hurts and I make love to him.

When it's over we're cold. I gather clumps of sawdust and pad the blankets with them for warmth, and, spent, he sleeps.

I don't. I try, but I can't.

The fourth cycle of Bob and Elise's divorce agreement had been scheduled to begin at the beginning of the July after Lars and Adam and John moved in. But as July approached, instead of packing her clothes and the silver, Elise had begun to spend her afternoons sunbathing in the narrow strip of deep-green yard between the house and the woods. In the pitch black of Los Anenomes I could see that yard as if I were standing in it. It was so narrow it stood in full sunlight only from noon to one-thirty—before that it was shadowed by the house; after, by the trees. In 1968, in suburbia, no other part of the property was secluded enough for a matron of thirty-three in a bikini.

At about eleven-thirty Elise would get out a plate of sandwiches, a tray of raw vegetables, and three individually wrapped Scooter Pies for Adam, John, and me. Then she would wander out the garage door with a bath towel just too small for comfortable sunbathing (the habit wasn't calculated enough to buy a beach towel), one back issue each of *Daedalus* and *Vogue* (the exact issue of each changed every few days), and a tube of Bain de Soleil.

I would watch her from the window as she walked slowly and deliberately to the center of the yard, spread the towel over the grass, and lay down with the slowness, dread, and pleasure of a woman settling into a very hot bath. She never seemed to get much color. In fact, the deep black-green of the trees and lawn made her look even whiter than she already was. But she lay there religiously until the oaks and dogwoods began to cast their spidery shadows over legs and arms and the phone began to ring.

One of the three of us would rise reluctantly from a book, a game, or a dish of soupy ice cream to answer it. Usually it was Bob, my father, on the other end, although sometimes it was a lawyer, or Lars. We would takes turns calling Elise through the screen windows. John thought nothing of it. He took the calls as though they were calls from any stranger, and went peacefully back to his game. But Adam mumbled into the phone and ventured into the backyard himself with their names, so he didn't have to send the names of the callers out through the air. After he delivered his message, he was likely to disappear into the woods for the rest of the afternoon, leaving his hand of the game undone. When it was my turn to deliver a message I would hover a moment, fascinated, behind the dark screen of wire mesh. Then I'd watch her rouse herself to a sitting position as quickly and completely as a cat and then briefly fix her eyes on an undetermined point in the distance before sauntering inside in nothing but her bi-kini.

That first call would daisy-chain into a second, then a third. Sometimes Elise eventually remembered to go outside to get the towel and magazines; other times they'd stay until after nightfall, flapping in the breeze.

For this was the second remarkable thing about that summer: as my mother, in her bathing suit, spoke on and on with The Lawyer and my father and Lars and God knows who else, she prepared dinner feasts which, for sheer succulence and visual beauty, I have never seen equaled.

Adam and I used to watch her: her face bloated by tears, her voice a hiss, her hands culling a mound of perfect, moist, moon-colored wedges from a bag of dusty potatoes. Later on she'd lay out the sterling and enlist the two of us to carry in casseroles of curried carrots, chops gently sautéed in subtle spices, and soft baked potatoes that crumbled in their jackets like delicate, aromatic tree bark as we sliced into them with her heavy knives.

The device succeeded, although it took me years to see it for what it was. When Lars came home to the house that was not his, the opulent smells and textures and the gleaming utensils so flattered and relieved him that he'd overlook his wife's telltale dreaminess.

Although my mother's behavior was captivating, I couldn't tolerate the boys' loud dinnertime voices and Lars's way of directing a meal which had been planned to victimize him. It was noisy and tiring. I ached for the long, violet fall evenings my father and I would spend in our backyard, looking for stars. You could see stars at our house you couldn't see in New York, or even in town.

One night, over fruit salad, I asked Lars what had happened to the house he had lived in with the boys in the city.

"His old company lent it to him," Elise answered. "When Lars left, he had to give it back."

"You shouldn't have asked that about our house," Adam said after dinner as we emptied the dishwasher together.

"This is my dad's house too, you know."

"My dad says this is my home to act as I please."

Just then, the two clean, steaming dinner plates I held in my hands slipped out of my grip and onto the floor. We both watched as they rolled around and around like quarters.

Adam looked at me with an expression of responsibility borrowed from the face of a museum guard. Then he picked up the plates, dried them until they shone, put them on their shelf, and closed the cabinet door.

After dinner, he and I would ride our bicycles up and down the driveway in the spill of the garage spotlight. Our bobbing reflectors would come closer and closer to each other, our bikes would angle in, and I would feel the asphalt against the cuff of my pants. Lars had warned us not to ride the main road at night, because it was dangerously curved. But sometimes Adam slipped out onto the road without warning and I would follow him, the air smelling of heat, birch, and honeysuckle; the night insects brushing our faces; the distinct, placed click of our bicycle spokes cutting the night like an idea falling into place.

We would ride together, spokes matching spokes. Sometimes I was afraid I would go as far as I could go and then have to take the dark and lonely road back myself while my stepbrother rode on without me. But he always turned back when I did, making sure to stay just behind me so I wouldn't fall away.

When we got back to the house it would be as if no time had passed at all. And as if no one had missed us. All the bare windows would be ablaze, and Lars and Elise, mournfully slow-dancing to the White Album, would greet Adam and me like old friends from their first marriages as we slipped upstairs.

The afternoon phone calls flowed into early August, long after my mother, Lars, and the boys should have been gone.

Then, around the fifteenth, Elise packed up my clothes and drove me to the rental house.

It happened so quickly I barely had time to say goodbye to Adam, who stood sullenly at the front door, his eyes glowing, as Elise pushed me into the backseat, locked all four doors, and drove slowly out of the driveway.

Once we were out of sight of the house she pulled over, smoothed my hair, and made sure my seat belt was tight.

"If men weren't all so damned STUPID," she said to me, rubbing a corner of my mouth clean with tissue. Then she started off down the street again at a reckless pace.

Trees and houses slipped by quietly on either side of the car, suspended in a lubricant of sunshine.

I said the only thing I could think of: "It's okay, Mom."

She was quiet after that. When I looked at her face in the rearview mirror I saw that she was crying.

When we stopped in front of the rental house Bob was standing in the front door. He didn't move as Elise got out of the car, pulled my two suitcases from the trunk, and stood me next to them on the sidewalk. Then she got back into the car, slid over to the passenger-side window, and rolled it all the way down.

"I can't help it," she whispered to me, in collusion, as though she and I shared a joke. Then she turned her face toward my father.

"I'll need the valise back," she trilled. "It belongs to Lars."

At the screen door, Bob flinched.

"I want it back," she said in tones as smooth and clear as glass. But her voice sounded thin and tinkly in the languid summer evening. Then she moved back to the driver's seat, wiped her eyes with Kleenex, fastened her seat belt, and sped off.

The moon is glinting off the edges of the broken glass that still clings to the window frames of the front room at Los Anenomes. It's interesting how the raw edges hold all the light; the smooth ones stay dark and clear. It's supposed to be the other way around: what's rough is said to absorb light, what's smooth to reflect it. But that's my mistake. Sharpness and roughness aren't the same, even though either can take you by surprise.

I wonder what would happen if I tried to lead the broken windows back together again. In the window on the far left, the remaining glass swoops out down the frame like a sail. In another, only triangles are left around the sides, like teeth, or the edge of a harlequin's costume.

Then I stop myself. It would hurt to work on these, I'd get little glass splinters in my hands. I'd get frustrated; there isn't equipment up here. It would also be tiring. Even if I had equipment, I'd have to take the frames out of the windows and lay them flat, and what glass is left inside would probably drop away.

I wonder, why can't I leave well enough alone?

The yard of the rental house was small, bright, and striped with beds of carefully nourished zinnias and phlox. There were also a few scraggly crabapple trees. We always contemplated them sadly, but since the house was not ours, it seemed pointless to tend them or plant anew; who would be around to take pleasure in their growth? I thought of Adam and John riding out the parched days in the cool, dark, endlessly fascinating shelter of my woods. When Elise made her daily call to me I could often hear them playing in the background, but she never put them on the phone and I didn't ask to speak with them.

After the first few days, I stopped asking Bob why I was with him and how long we would be staying in the rental house. The few questions I did venture had been met with mysterious replies like, "Your mother has to make some hard decisions," or, "I'd rather be there, too."

Bob was much quieter than Elise. He had taken some vacation time when I arrived and disappeared after lunch to answer the calls Elise and the lawyers made, discreetly shutting the study door behind him. When he wasn't on the phone or doing errands he taught me how to play badminton in the sun.

I liked playing badminton better than most other pastimes because it kept me from noticing things. For instance, I knew that Elise had always hated the isolation and darkness of the house on the hill and struggled defiantly to get her daily hour in the sun. Meanwhile, I noticed, Bob was always asking the gardener at the rented house to grow flowers that would somehow become as dense and alluring as our oaks and pines and dogwood trees. It made me uncomfortable to realize each of my parents had trapped the other in the place they wanted for themselves.

Bob and I always picked up our badminton racquets without mentioning the delicate and painful telephone conversations that had such a direct bearing on my immediate future. He'd begin tapping the shuttlecock at me; first slowly, then faster. "Good Tessy, good Tessy, hey, yeah," he'd croon.

The lightness of the shuttlecock and the racquet always hypnotized me. So did the way I reassured him when I succeeded, even when the shuttlecock went un-

derneath the net instead of over the top. He never noticed when I got tired. The white blur went tap-tap-
tap and flew off again into the sunlight. It bounced off
the edge of my racquet and dribbled along the pole to
the ground. My father would snatch it up and lob. We
kept at it.

"Higher! Closer! Faster!" he'd direct. Sometimes,
tears would begin to slip down my cheeks. Bob went
on serving and the little white shuttlecock would waver
its arc into the hot sun and I tried hard, hard, hard to
give it back to him, this precious little white-winged
thing he was entrusting me with. As I ran I'd think of
Adam and John exploring the cool, dark, wondrous
places I had shared with them.

"Come on, honey," Bob said one day. "You'll feel
better if you just keep on going."

◇

It wasn't until the end of August that I looked up from
the bright, bare yard, and the bright, bare house and
tried to remember what had happened to my friends.
Summer vacations always edited them away, but the
perpetually shifting foundation of my homelife made
uneasy shelter for children unfamiliar with such stir-
rings, and who knew to avoid me. How could I palm
off something I myself did not understand? At least
Adam and John and I had shared this astonishing experience. But now they lived in my house and I was
exiled.

I missed them.

The Sunday after Elise left me at Bob's doorstep he
relinquished me for a visit to the house on the hill. I
saw how Adam's slippers were neatly aligned at the
foot of my bed, how Adam's microscope and slide trays
covered my desk, how his books were scattered across
my bedroom floor, and my feelings changed.

I didn't feel like talking much at dinner.

Periodically, Adam interrupted his excited tales of cells and onion skins to look at me with eyes that were both fascinated and terrified.

I told Bob I would not like to go back again.

◊

By Labor Day it seemed as if everyone had left town or forgotten about Bob and me.

That Friday the phone calls stopped and the two of us packed our suitcases, got into the car, and drove to a motel on the water. Inland there was a piney mountain with two restaurants and four dirt trails. At the top of the shortest trail was a field and a lookout post covered with sharp gravel that dated from Colonial times. It was a popular place for stargazing. Bob and I sat in the last row of benches, facing out over the lookout point, as an authority on astronomy from New York described the meteor showers in a sober, gravelly voice.

After the lecture, Bob opened up the little wooden case he had been carrying. Inside was a small gray telescope with a band of darker gray around the lens.

I didn't quite know what to make of it.

"Here," Bob said. "This is for you."

I held the cold tube in my hands. It felt heavy. It was about the length of my forearms, and it had a little silver knob on its underside with what looked like a keyhole on the end. All I could think was why anyone would want to unlock a telescope.

"Don't you like it?" my father asked.

"Yes," I said.

He looked at me suspiciously. Then he put one hand on my shoulders and led me toward the edge of the lookout, where the American rebels had spotted Tory soldiers. There he took his gift from my hands and held it up to his eye. If in my hands the telescope had seemed too large and heavy, against my father's brow poised skyward, it seemed absurdly small. He fidgeted for a long time with the lens opening, and then he stood perfectly still. He turned the focus back and forth so slowly I thought he had forgotten I was there. And he seemed to be bracing his face against an impact, as if instead of a telescope he held a rifle.

Finally, he knelt on the ground, squinted through the eyepiece one last time, and presented the telescope to me.

"Look over there," he said, pointing the tube almost straight ahead, toward a spot of sky close to the horizon. I looked. I felt uncomfortable. Lars had taken the boys and me to the Planetarium over the winter and I had felt like an outsider. While the three of them had exclaimed gleefully over the beautiful women, archers, beasts, fowl, and fish the stars made I had seen nothing but bright dots with lines drawn between them at unnatural angles.

"Can't you see," Lars had said gently, sensing I was new at this game he and his sons had been practicing for some time, "there is her hair, there is her brush, and there, her other hand, holding the mirror." He pointed in the air and traced shapes with his fingers.

When I saw what he meant, I was astounded. The five little stars on the ceiling bore little resemblance to the beautiful woman Lars was describing. In a bewildering and terrifying burst of insight I beheld an unbroken chain of fathers and sons playing this game with the same fixed collection of images; a precise, collective hallucination.

Mutely, I simply nodded yes. I sat back, and felt despair. For the rest of the show, awestruck, I had watched the huge, listing contraption of silver globes and rods that cast the night sky onto the dome. I was almost afraid to know how it worked. And I had even been relieved when I asked Lars and he couldn't tell me.

Cautiously, I put my eye to the lens of the telescope my father had given to me.

"Do you see Pegasus?" he said. "It's that big kite in the middle of the sky."

The opening at the end of the telescope was very small. I saw the sky, and an airplane, and a smattering of stars that reminded me vaguely of a flock of birds. I shook my head.

Bob knelt down beside me. It seemed to be very important to him that I saw what he did when he looked through. His concern made me feel very important, and very sorry that I didn't see what he wanted me to, and confused. He took the telescope from me, pointed it at the sky, and moved it back and forth for a while. Finally, like a deer in the moment before it bolts, he froze.

"Come stand where I am," he said, "and take the telescope."

I obeyed.

"Now do you see it?" It was a rhetorical question.

And I did see it. It looked most like a kite, but I saw how the tail of the kite could also be the head and neck of a horse.

At the corner opposite the kite tail or horse head, two strings of stars dangled.

"The kite even has strings," I said.

Bob was silent for a minute.

"Oh, that's Andromeda," he finally said.

I asked him who that was.

"A beautiful woman whose mother boasted about her. She was almost sacrificed, but a man named Perseus rescued her, and she had a long and happy life. So happy, that when she died, she became those stars in the heavens. It's not easy to see Andromeda," he finished almost apologetically.

I tried and tried, but all I could see were strings. Maybe the strings were really hair. It was getting cold.

My father cleared his throat.

"Do you see the bright star in the corner of Pegasus that ties the strings together?"

I said I did.

"Even though it's the brightest, Pegasus and Andromeda share that star. It's part of both constellations at the same time. Neither of them would be the same without it," he finished triumphantly. "Now isn't that something?"

I knew what he was getting at. But I didn't want to talk about it.

I gave the telescope back to him.

He pushed it back at me.

"It's yours," he said.

I carried the telescope and he carried the box as we walked over the gravel-covered lookout and back to the car.

◇

Adam and I had different last names and we were assigned to the same sixth-grade class.

On the first day of school we went to opposite corners of the room and pretended not to know each other. A few of our friends knew the truth. But our exotic situation chastened them, and they did not betray us.

Our teacher noticed nothing. When Miss Frome observed the giggles and furtive stares that passed through the classroom when she called my name and Adam's every morning she may have assumed this was just an example of children's naturally sparse sense of propriety. But whatever the cause, she was too involved in herself to find Adam and me out. At first the joke had been a good one, and our misidentification by the world of grown-ups too awesomely curious to correct.

But time went on. And the longer it went on, the harder it became to tell Miss Frome the truth, because her anger was mighty and her prejudices long-lived. She taught as though goodness were a religion and the few children still born into it did not believe.

I think we were both dismayed.

We tried hard not to look at each other in class or in study group.

At lunch, we would sometimes exchange a hostile word or two outside the cafeteria, sometimes even just a push, and then disappear inside to our separate friends. *"Who cares anyway,"* Adam hissed on the blacktop. *"You get your grades. I get mine. What does she have to know?"*

At home it was just as easy. From time to time Bob quizzed me on my school day with a mildly solicitous but absent air. Historically, school went effortlessly with me, and I think he felt relieved that there was one area of my life to which he did not have to give the bright, minute attention he conscientiously applied to the rest. I was quietly amazed at my ability to pull off such a feat, yet perplexed by my inability to share it.

Bob never asked about John or about Adam. When I mentioned them, his chin seemed to get sharper out of restrained interest, and his eyes got a certain look. We had both learned not to talk of my stepbrothers.

I never found out what Adam said at home. Nor did I really care to think about it too deeply, because the idea of him so guiltlessly deceiving my mother in that way boys had so dismayed me.

I was sure I'd be found out when I had my first visit

with Elise after school started. Elise's questions were as artful as a gifted surgeon's incisions: sure and narrow and deep.

She picked me up on Saturday as usual, slightly wilted yet proud from the effort of having pulled herself away from the men and the house on such a strategic, errand-running day.

But when we finally sat together over blueberry pancakes in town, I noticed for the first time that just as a solid turns into a liquid, and a liquid turns into a gas, my warrior mother had receded into a distant, silvery person who talked like little bells, drummed her index fingers against the table, and never once asked a single question of content—such as, who was my teacher.

And so I felt the glee and horror of having the earth pulled out from under me just to find I could stand quite securely in the sky.

◊

I heard Adam's low whistle behind me one morning on the way to class.

"Essa," I heard. "Essa, ess, Mess, Vanessa."

I turned around. He was standing on fresh sod labeled PLEASE DON'T WALK ON ME.

"*Vanessa.* Why don't they ever call you by your real name?" he asked suspiciously. The tips of his ears were bright red.

"When I was little I didn't like 'Nessa. And I was just learning how to read and I read the word 'Tess' on the cover of a book because it was like my name. Dad said it suited me better than the name of a monster anyway, and Mom said not to scare me."

Adam stuck his jaw into the air. "What monster?" he said.

"I don't know," I blurted, furious for letting so much escape at once after weeks of silence.

Adam just stared at me as the other children walked into the classroom.

"I know which monster," he announced calmly. "The Loch Ness monster. It lives at the bottom of a lake in Scotland and sometimes it comes up to the surface. Some people think it's real and some people don't."

I was silent.

"Do you remember that happening? With the book, I mean?"

"Yes," I lied. Really I didn't recall any of it. I remembered pointing out the book, but not the monster. Elise started to explain that later, to new friends, at parties.

Adam walked right up to me, close. He peered into my face. "Let's wait till the end of the year," he suggested. "When we get our final report cards. We can call a conference and announce it. And show how jerky they are."

"Okay," I said slowly. "But what about your brother?"

"He's in," Adam said solemnly. "When they find out they'll do all sorts of things for us."

"The heck they will," I said. "They'll be mad."

"Nah," he said, peering into my face. "They might even buy you a tent, or a telephone."

"No, they won't."

"My dad did when you left."

"We have to swear not to tell," I said firmly.

"Blood oath."

I pulled a pin out of my jacket pocket.

Adam shook his head briefly: a blip of emotion on that cool, detached screen. He touched his hip and I saw the Swiss Army knife there. He gestured toward the side of the building. And there, in the shade, we did it.

"Adam and Tessy sitting in a tree . . ." we heard from the sidewalk.

"Vamos," said Adam.

Pressing the blood back into our fingers, we slipped in the cafeteria door.

◊

"Hey, Bob," I said the next week on Saturday.

"Yes, sweets."

He was in the yard clipping back the cherry trees and I had come up from behind. Bob had a distinctive gardening style. He always looked very still and poised; almost formal, rather like a crane, yet his attention would be so deep his face would crinkle and pull and show every move and decision he made.

"Can I have a kaleidoscope?"

The elbows and neat nape stayed perfectly in place as he said, "But why not the telescope, sweets? That's a real kaleidoscope. You don't need any tricks for that."

I knew my prey.

"We saw a movie about prisms and light," I said. "I wanted to see. Try for myself, I mean. That's all."

He turned around and smiled at me, that wonderful, sad, piercing smile.

"That's a perfectly marvelous idea. But let's get you into the Planetarium at the University one night to look through the big telescope, too."

Adam's right, I thought, as I stumbled back to my room.

Exactly one Saturday later at breakfast I found a blue cardboard kaleidoscope and the added treat of a fat, shiny prism on my plate. Bob had been out with his friend Esther the night before. Esther had black hair, red cheeks, deep, Indian-cottoned cleavage, and a slightly gap-toothed smile. Bob did some research with her at the school and I wondered if she had helped him pick out my present, although I didn't ask.

After breakfast Elise called and drew Bob away.

The kaleidoscope was disappointing. Within its orb, everything was rendered to a uniform opacity and the same lines and planes repeated endlessly. I plotted and angled for variety, only to have my most inspired schemes replicate the same patterns again and again and again. The only time it was any better was when I aimed the cylinder at someone and caught tiny, slivered duplicates suspended in that geometric sea. I was fascinated by the way the tiny people could look so correctly placed, yet at the same time so lost and trivial.

But the prism held a special discovery. I loved the way something that felt so fat and cold could reduce the world to smears of colored incandescence when held to the eye, to one tender, fleeting screen of light. It too reduced the world to a single view, yet in contrast to the perspective the kaleidoscope gave, this one seemed to pose and solve a mystery at the same time.

Now that I understood nothing would happen to us, I could take my place in class just like any other student. My terror returned only when Miss Frome would walk in and begin to recite the pledge of allegiance. I knew that meant attendance would follow, and with it that brief powderflash of mass scrutiny. But disaster never struck. Every day that little window of danger closed behind us.

And when we had to draw partners for the Columbus Day Discovery Fair in Science, I drew Adam.

We hadn't spoken much since the day we sealed our pact, more, I think, out of fear of being labeled a hot romance than for fear of being found out.

When we broke up into partners during science class to discuss our assignment—Adam and I had drawn chemistry—I found him skulking in a corner.

"Don't worry," he assured me, brushing a lock of flaxen hair out of his eye. "They won't ask you anything. They're too busy looking at their own belly buttons. They won't even come."

"Hey, Bob," I said that night over dinner. "When are we going back to the big house?"

My father blinked slowly, as if waking up, even though he had been just about to bite into a barbecued pork chop. Loving the outdoors as he did, even at the small rental house Bob insisted on cooking out until the snow started to fall. He had cooking mitts of different weights for different weather, and he changed from one to the next as smoothly and precisely as he measured chemicals for lab experiments.

"It isn't certain," said Bob.

"Before the next meteor shower in the fall?"

"We can get a great view of the stars at Esther's observatory," Bob pointed out.

"Do I have to go back there in February anyway?"

"Do you want to?" He looked at me intently, sideways.

"I want to live in our house." But even as I said this I felt a shadow descend on the house on the hill. I couldn't say what kind of shadow, but there it was.

"Succotash," Bob said, and served us both some.

This response annoyed me.

"I have a new chemistry project," I announced.

"What is it?" he said. He seemed surprised but mildly relieved by the change in direction.

"Don't know. Have to choose."

"Choose what?"

"I have to show how something was discovered," I said. "Something chemical."

"Does it have to be a chemical?"

"No. Just a chemical change." I lingered over those new words authoritatively. In class, I had been intrigued by them while Adam had seen them as nothing more than the next step in his plan to humiliate all significant adults.

"A chemical change." Deftly, Bob coaxed some succotash onto his fork. He smiled a little, and then his eyes became remote, resting on the prism that was on a shelf behind me. "Why don't you do a report on the discovery of optical glass," he said, "and on the manufacture of prisms?" He looked back at me shyly and smiled a little more.

My face went blank. It was one thing to love the pictures the prism made when I looked through it, but it was quite another to report on the hard science that made all those wonderful, mystical images happen. It was like taking the air out of the balloon.

Bob must have noted my crestfallen expression. "Someone discovered glass in very ancient times. They were burning a very hot fire on a beach, and the sand and the ash burned so hot they liquefied and ran clear. Like a river in the sand. And when it cooled, they had something clear and hard and shining. Like ice that would never melt. That's how it started. Something like that."

"How could ashes make something so clear?"

He smiled. "Ah. That is one of the natural miracles. And these days they make windows by floating the hot liquid on top of a tank of mercury, then cooling it down. All hot and silver. Only way they can make sure the glass is completely even. Like the little water gauge in my carpenter's level. Know what I mean?"

"So the mercury is like the mercury in the thermometer," I said slowly, "so it doesn't freeze and it doesn't boil if it reaches very high degrees. So that's why they use it instead of water."

He nodded. "Also, it's heavy, so it holds the glass up

that way. And when the liquid glass cools and hardens,
the mercury is still liquid, so they just move it away."

My mind was reeling, captured by the look and feel
of that wonderfully artificial, upside-down but perfectly logical arrangement my father was describing.

"But that doesn't have anything to do with prisms,"
I said.

"No, Tess," said Bob. "You're right. That's a different process."

"What's that?" I cried.

He leaned back and crossed his arms, but his eyes
were still soft. "Do your project and find out," he said.
Then he winked.

◇

But real choice was much more subtle than that.

Miss Frome took our suggestions in our next science
class. Adam and I watched her columns of yellow-chalk
words blister up the blackboard. The way things
worked in Miss Frome's class, teams were obligated to
offer up topics to the classroom, whose silent scrutiny
would, apparently, bring any lurking unsoundness to
her diamond-hard attention.

"Tess J. and Adam M.," she called out eventually.

We had not conferred privately on the subject. We
had tried, but we had both felt sullen and thick.

"Optical glass," I called out.

She blinked at me as if she hadn't heard what I had
said.

"Adam M."

"Uhm, what about the origin of the chemical elements? The way the explosion of the stars started the
heavy ones, all the elements as we know them, and how
before that, in those stars, all they have are light gases?
We could do a mural about the birth of the elements."

Miss Frome leaned against a desk in the front row

with the hand that wasn't holding the chalk. She blinked several times, as if a bright light stood between her and us.

"Your subgroup is chemistry, is it not, Adam M.?"

"Yes, Miss Frome."

"Very well, then. The Galaxy of Chemicals is your topic. Optical glass is perhaps a subject better suited to the physics group." She wrote *Galaxy Chem.* in her column and straightened up to greet her next group of supplicants.

To while away the rest of the class period, he drew an exploding star surrounded by tender, newborn, burning planets. *CO_2,* he wrote. *Cu. Fe. H_2SO_4.*

◇

On Columbus Day, our classroom became a fair. Adam was smug: Elise and Lars were out of town together on a long weekend in Vermont. I was smugger: that morning, Bob told me he was taking an hour off from work to come on by, but I hadn't told Adam yet.

We stood in front of the mural we had made: Incandescent golden spheres lobbed balls of fire out of the universe. Planets cooled, their colors deepened, and outlines became crisper, more intense. Life formed, bearing heavier nuclei, gloriously differentiated elements which we had listed in crisp black pen overhead. The more life differentiated, the more kinds of raw substance formed, and the more there was to delight in. Working on the mural, it had all come together.

"Ho, Tess," I heard. It was Bob behind me.

"Hi, Daddy," I said, shy and prickling with secret anticipation. Adam would see. He would see.

"Gee," Bob said. "This is a beauty." He stooped and ran his hands over one yellow energy source, brushing it off.

"Three coats of paint," Adam announced, walking up

behind Bob. "But not too thick, or they crack. Adam Martinson," he concluded heartily, extending his hand.

Astonished, I watched Bob regard this small boy suddenly turned conventioneer. More than anything, Bob looked amused.

"Robert Jordan," he replied solemnly.

"Are you the guy with the telescopes?" Adam asked.

Bob nodded, putting his right hand on my shoulder. I could see the other kids in our class dotted around the room in similar scenarios. But not entirely similar. Bob bent down closer to my eye level and singsonged in my general earshot, "We've seen aster-oids, and Peg-asus, and even some nifty nebulae." Then he winked. At both of us. I recoiled.

"Wow! I'd really like to see some sometime."

"Tessy's telescope is in the car," Bob said. "Maybe after the fair we can all take a look at it."

Adam gave me a shifty little triumphant glance.

"Adam lives in our house, Daddy," I said.

"Yeah, I gathered. So they let you work on this project together?"

"We're in the *same class,*" I said.

"Yes. I'm sure Adam is a very good student too," said my father.

"That's not what I meant."

He turned to me and mussed my hair with one hand.

"I know what you meant."

Then he turned and mussed Adam's hair, too.

Adam's eyes glinted strangely.

So the three of us spent that afternoon taking apart my telescope and putting it back together again. Since it was daytime, once the thing was assembled, we could use it only to look at trees, cars, pavements, and each other.

But that was plenty.

That night Bob said, "I suppose they put you in that class together by accident."

I nodded.

"What's a year?" Bob said. "Next year they'll know better. Next year we'll all know better."

"It's okay."

"Yes. It is."

But at that moment what he had told me about the sand and ash heating and clearing and blending into each other was blended into me, in turn, forever.

"The universe isn't expanding anymore," I informed my father. "It's contracting now."

CHAPTER EIGHT

◇

Los Anenomes at night seems blacker than other houses. I take my bearings in sound: the poplar trees clicking in the wind; Javier's regular breath. This is the first night I've spent away from my apartment since I came to Begar. It feels like a single night spent away from home, instead of one of many nights on the road, distinct and full of possibility. The new perspective has livened my senses, I can't stop it. Everything begins to look fresh from here. In this new frame, what I know begins to recompose.

◇   ◇   ◇

This is Adam Martinson, my high school friend Karen said.

The night was black, black, and the swimming pool

diamond bright. I wanted to scream. Behind Adam and Karen the windows of Karen's house were as bright as the pool. The shadows of other teenagers moved in and out of them. The rest of the kids were in the house; on the porch; magnetized to the edge of the pool.

I was fifteen; Adam sixteen. I hadn't seen him in four years. He and John had gone to live with their mother in New York before I returned to the house in the woods once Bob and Elise finally agreed to keep the homes they were in, but to share me. Adam had just left for Mariah's and refused to return, and suddenly Lars would not see him either. Elise told me it was because she and Adam hadn't gotten along and I wondered if she might have treated him coldly during my absence. But all I knew for sure was that by the time Bob gave me up, Adam was gone.

Some boys are at their most beautiful in early adolescence, but Adam's looks had been spoiled. His cheeks looked dirty and his eyes were frightened. Yet from the way Karen curved her neck toward him, I could tell girls liked him anyway.

"Hi," I said easily.

It was the trick of the last names again.

"Pleased to meet you," he said back. He held his head very still as he spoke. But his eyes lost that fear and went calm.

It was easy to keep up the charade, both out of embarrassment and out of a sense of adventure, just as we had kept up that other charade as children.

"I know Adam from the city," Karen trilled. "His mama's my modern teacher. Dance, you know. Not life, ha ha."

Just then someone called to Karen from inside the swimming-pool fence.

Adam looked off into the distance and his eyes fluttered in that way they'd always had when the gears were turning. He began to speak, and before he could get one word out I was convinced he was going to try to get away from me.

And I had just discovered I didn't want him to.

"Want something to drink?" I nodded toward the lit picture window at the back of Karen's house. There was a deck, and a door, and kids I knew from school were coming in and out. It occurred to me Adam must hardly know anyone at the party. "I was on my way there," I went on. "My friends are back at the pool." I thought of the strange way flesh lit up in a swimming pool at night as it moved through the bright water with black all around: opaque, like a costume, even though you felt more vulnerable and exposed than you did swimming during the day. I was a thin person, but I still didn't like the feeling. So I'd been happy to get the drinks for the rest.

"Okay then," said Adam.

In the living room, everyone was pairing off. Cigarettes were floating slowly in the air and hands were moving fast. The table that served as the bar was sticky. We each had a beer. We turned around side by side and leaned against the table. He was almost a full head taller than I was. All I could think about was how his Adam's apple stuck out, and how funny this was because of his name. And I could hear his slow, soft breathing. That comforted me, because otherwise he seemed so defenseless and far away.

"What about your friends?" Adam said.

I shrugged. I had no desire to go back to the pool.

"You go to school with Karen?" he asked.

"Yeah."

"Mariah let me stay the weekend. She doesn't know Karen's 'rents are away."

"You goin' with Karen, then?"

"Nuh. She's a nice girl. But her mom and my mom just go way back. High school or something."

"Well, I don't really want to go back to the pool now if you know what I mean."

Adam gestured vaguely.

"Karen's brother and some other guy's girlfriend were making out together at the edge."

"In the water?"

"In the deep end. *Really* deep, you know?"

He looked at me curiously.

I rolled my eyes in response and he broke out in a wide grin.

"Kind of desperate, you suburb kids, huh? I guess I shouldn't have bothered with my bathing suit." He pointed his chin at the scene before us.

Couples were melting into corners and slipping up the stairs. Mostly, they faced the wall, studious in their tasks.

Just then my friends at the pool burst into the door, draped in bathing suits and towels. Another friend, Liz, began to make a beeline toward me, already chiding and chattering over the lost beers. But when she saw Adam her eyes narrowed and she faded off to the left with the rest.

None of this had escaped him.

Karen was at the top of the stairs, making her way down.

"Want to stroll a little?" he asked abruptly.

"Yeah, sure," I answered, not sure at all.

I followed him out the door.

The night was even blacker now and emptied of all

sound but the luscious hum of crickets. I stepped on a paper cup and listened to its shape hiss away into air.

Adam turned a sharp left and headed toward the woods at the edge of the yard.

"No," I called sharply. He looked back over his shoulder at me. His startled face was shadowed with guilt.

"What about a swim?" I suggested softly.

I waited for him to catch up to me and we walked silently to the shining rectangle.

As I lifted my cover-up over my head, I felt a chill on my shoulders and legs. It was the wind playing across the moisture that still clung from my last swim.

"I'm going in," I yelled, jumping.

Adam stood above. For a minute I thought he might turn and leave, and part of me wished he would. After all, there is something indulgent about choosing to be without. If he had walked away, at least part of me would have been relieved.

But Adam walked over to the deep end. He took off his shirt and his jeans. He was wearing loose, bright-orange swimming trunks. Without a word he began to swim laps. His stroke started slow, and grew faster.

I followed his lead, starting from the shallow end of the pool. For a while we just passed each other in opposite directions. The water was so bright and cold it knocked out all other feelings like an antiseptic and I thought of the pitchers of gin and tonics from that slow, sad summer so long ago. We swam silently and intently for perhaps fifteen minutes, our only communication in our abrupt changes of direction, splashes, and the low drag of our bodies' wake.

I tried to forget the way flesh looked in the water. I wanted to forget I had a body.

Instead, even worse, I imagined how I might feel when he pulled himself out of the water and watched me.

One of us had to stop swimming first. I didn't want to be the one left stroking halfheartedly through the blue, so I hooked my arms around the pool side and followed him with my eyes. Still cool as a cucumber, he was now displayed to me in the bright frame of water.

Within a lap or two he retreated from a noisy crawl to a slow breaststroke.

"Sounds like some people are leaving," I remarked.

"How can you tell?" he gasped.

"Cars."

"You have a car?"

"No. You're different, you know, than you were."

"Different? How?"

"Just different."

"Well, you're the same." The strokes were even slower now.

"I am?" I said. "How?"

"Oh. Soft and tough at the same time. Like a shark's tooth in a piece of taffy."

"Since when are you the poet?"

He had stopped now and hooked his arms around the pool side opposite me.

"I do some reading," he said quietly. His mouth was open a little and he was looking at the choker I always used to wear. Gold, with a gold leaf hanging from it. "Doesn't that rust in the water?" he asked.

"No. Why would it?"

"It's real, then." He sounded defeated.

"Yeah, it's real."

There was a glimmer in his eyes—of annoyance? at-

traction? It wasn't until I visited Mariah's apartment
that I would understand it was of jealousy and wistful-
ness.

"So what do you like to read?" I asked to keep the
stillness moving.

"Philosophy. Science. I bet you put lemon juice in
your hair," he added.

"What about it?"

"Nothing. I could guess what music you listen to. I
bet you take ballet with Karen. I bet you're still good
at school."

"I bet you like me more than you used to."

I swam out into the middle of the pool and floated
on my back. Again, I thought of the way my hair
looked streaming out around me, and how my new
breasts floated above the waterline. No matter what, I
felt completely insulated.

When I opened my eyes Adam was standing on the
grass right above me and looking down.

"Let's go," he said. "It's getting cold."

As I climbed out he threw me a towel.

We wrapped up and went back to the house. Inside,
all the lights were off. The party was almost over, but
everyone left was entangled in a pair in a corner or on
a couch. The air was thick with clumsy desire. Even
with the music playing, the room seemed silent with
intense focus. Adam and I started to stifle giggles. Wet
and shivering, we retreated to the top of the stairs. Soon
we were both doubled over and shaking with laughter
and cold.

"Let's go back out again," he whispered.

"Okay," I whispered back. "But don't trip over anyone."

This time we walked around in back of the pool to

the place where there was a hedge and a fence. Images of what I'd just seen interlaced with scenes from my imagination. I felt Adam breathing at my side. I remembered how the two of us had used to avert our eyes when we came upon Elise and Lars kissing. And how our eyes used to flick by each other's anyway.

We put our towels down. At that moment, I realized, I felt very close to him. I remembered the way I'd seen him looking at me while I floated on my back in the pool. I felt giddy, safe, free.

Without another word, I began stripping off my bathing suit. I started laughing, and twirled around.

"Is *this* the way you remember me?" The black night cloaking me was friendly, beckoning. I put my arms over my head and shook like a belly dancer. I put my hand to my choker. I looked up at the thick night and the gleaming stars. I lay down on my towel and demurely turned my head away. Somewhere far away in the front of the yard I could heard a muffled moan and whispers.

At first I heard nothing and I sucked in my breath. Then came slow footsteps on the grass. He knelt down and touched my side with one finger. It was a soft touch, so soft that for a moment I was afraid for him. But then he turned my head back to meet his eyes and held it there. We looked at each other as slowly he ran his other hand the length of my body. Then he took my hand and traced circles with it on his body. We were both smiling. Then we were clinging together on the green turf as the bracing water lapped along in the background.

We shook ourselves dry and turned away from each other to dress. Then we exchanged a series of mumbles and gestures, and took off down the middle of the deserted road with our hands at our sides and without saying where we were walking to. Eventually we found ourselves turning onto the road that led to Elise's house. Still, we neither spoke nor stopped. As we moved closer, I began to watch to see what would change in him as we approached the house where his father still lived, if he would crack at all as I disappeared into the yellow light, the protected space where his father was sleeping, unaware, or, even worse, waiting up for me. It seemed Adam might have begun to carry himself a little more carefully, as if he were a glassful of something about to spill over, but I couldn't be sure if this was truth or wishfulness. Whatever it was, it seemed only to heighten our spell of desire and surrender.

At the foot of the driveway I turned to him. His eyes flared with a little of that astonished look, that look I would get to know so well yet never point out. I felt tough then, and I knew there was something left to conquer before I could say goodnight. But he was the one who swooped lips down to my neck and my ear and whispered, even though there was no one to hear him, *Mom teaches all day Saturdays.*

He left me there with that. He blinked as if to rouse himself and then walked away.

As I put my hand on the doorknob, I heard footsteps running up the street behind me. I turned to save him, to block him, to protect our night.

However it was not Adam but his father who ran toward me through the velvety black, his eyes glazed, his chest naked and heaving. My first thought was that we had been followed, and discovered. But then I realized that Lars did not even see me. He was absorbed in his exertion, and mumbling to himself.

I hesitated, then stepped behind the rhododendron to

the side of the door and waited for him to tear past. It had to be midnight. I weighed the odds of his having seen Adam, and what I would say if he had. When what seemed like a safe interval had passed I peered through the living room window.

The room itself was dark. But in the square frame of light that was the kitchen beyond, I could see him, still shirtless, removing all the utensils from their drawers and sorting them on the table. Either we had been discovered, or he and my mother had argued. I felt a hot ball of arrogance inside. I strode in the door and began to walk upstairs.

"Hi there, Tess," I heard. He sounded loud, sardonic, knowing. Not at all like the reserved, thoughtful man we knew.

"Hello," I said. Lars's hands kept moving quickly. It was as if he were sorting out sharp feelings and thoughts along with knives and scrapers and slotted spoons. His mouth was closed in a funny way.

"What are you doing there?" he said in the same voice. "It's late."

"I had to wait for my ride."

No response. He gave me one more quick glance. He swore to himself. Then in one movement he dismissed me, spun back to a set of kitchen knives, and swept them all into the sink with the back of his hand.

I was speechless.

"All right, all right already," he said, rummaging through the sinkful of knives with his bare hands. "Go to bed."

I went.

Had he seen us? Or hadn't he? I didn't want to think about what Lars's silence meant in either case. So instead I decided not to think at all.

Upstairs, as I walked past her door, I heard Elise humming sad songs.

I saw nothing but Adam walking, walking back alone along the dark road to Karen's house as I waited for sleep to take me.

I could still see him walking through the night as Elise and I ate pancakes the next morning. Elise seemed unusually distracted, and kept patting her hair, as if it were about to come undone, although she had actually pinned it up much more neatly than usual. She said nothing about the piles of utensils, which she and I had moved aside so we could eat. During the night they had been joined by a glossy mountain of pots and pans.

Lars emerged shortly. Elise ran to his side, whispering and proffering juice and a selection of vitamins. Then they went off for a drive. At dinnertime they came back relaxed, smiling, and bearing summer fruit, and I knew the danger had passed.

It wasn't until later that I would find out that the real discovery to be made that night was not Lars's but mine.

But as I drifted into sleep that night, Adam was still walking through my thoughts to an unfamiliar house, and now Lars was running after him.

CHAPTER NINE

◇

I wake up first.

I'm at Los Anenomes and it's morning. Light has come back into the world. I'm looking at pieces of wire, and sun pouring through wooden slats. Between them parts of the same unrecognizable words repeat themselves over and over again.

A hand is gripping one of my hips.

For a moment, I just lie there silently. Then Javier shrugs in his sleep and moves his hand away.

I pull myself up and sit against a crate, blinking. Through the windows I see Luis carrying cans of paint across the slope toward the boat. Even at the end of summer the trees and fields appear tender with renewal. Oblivious to all the human tumult unfolding on their slopes, they give off sanctuary the way flowers give off scent. The white-green early-morning light bathes me in calm.

I feel safe, simplified. I'm in a world made out of a limited palette of beautiful colors which still somehow reproduce every possible shade. I can't recall feeling so quiet.

It's time for Javier to admit he is awake.

"Why is it that I feel like I could stay right exactly here for as long as I wanted until I found just the right time and place to sneak back into the world? Without anyone noticing. It's like I've given the world the slip and I'm on the balcony enjoying the view." I pause. "Is that how you felt in the mountains?"

He shifts a little, and rubs his eyes.

"No. No time to. But if there had been I might have."

I knew he'd wake as soon as I moved. I'd known the night before when I saw him slip the knife in the leather sheath out of his clothes and into one of the boots that stood next to the bed. Interesting, he hasn't noticed I mentioned the mountains that are part of his secret.

"It's very soothing," I say, fully aware of the knife-edge my words walked but feeling I must share them with him, to show we could talk about the part of his life he'd touched on that morning in his apartment. "In fact, I could see how a person could end up feeling very superior to all those people down on the coast toiling away at their little lives. I wonder if that's how the ladies who used to come here felt."

"Those poor women locked up by their lazy sons-of-whores husbands," Javier replies. "To shit, they felt superior."

"Yeah. But I bet some got here on their own. I think they knew they'd hit the jackpot."

He leans up on his elbow, reaches into the boot, and puts the knife back into a pocket. "My country is a lunatic who locks his sons and daughters up in other men's castles." This, with a mixture of dry annoyance and pride. "Never tell me I planned to be here."

"But it's so special here."

"You're just like Maite." He pulls on his boots. "She was always finding something good about everything." He sounds incredulous.

We are silent.

"You are not like Maite in most other ways," he says.

"How so?"

"In precisely that way you could not be more different."

"You mean because I ask questions."

"No, because some things you must find out without asking questions."

"I think I've already given you the great courtesy of not asking the most important questions."

"You wouldn't enjoy knowing."

"Give me the choice."

"It's not your struggle." He lingers over the final word as if it were the last sip of a rare and particularly beloved wine.

"Maybe not that way," I say quietly. "But here I am. You drove me halfway. Maybe I came the rest of the way myself, but without you I never would have started."

"I never meant you to follow."

"Didn't you?"

He's angry.

"No."

"That isn't so," I say. "I believe you wanted a witness. Maybe you didn't realize it, but I think that's what you wanted."

"You think I just want a witness." He still sounds incredulous. The dark look comes over him and I'm sorry I've spoken. He turns away from me. "A witness is not part of the struggle."

"And a lover?"

"Don't be romantic."

"Who is the romantic here?"

Just then, as suddenly as the early-morning sun pierced the room, Javier lights again. His face softens and he seems to step toward me and step away at the same time. The secret he knows, his expression says, makes my fear of him ludicrous, and why don't I see it too. But then he recedes to his usual half-light and half-shadow, and whatever it is he began to say hangs there latent. He thwacks one of the cases and chuckles.

"It's done. You're here. You can't undo it. I can't undo it. But I cannot explain what is done, either. Will you commit acts as grave as those I have committed? Of course not. Are you safe? Am I safe? No one is safe. But it is better right now that you stay. Until the next step. If you knew what we were about and one of the *locos* found out . . ." Javier's words trail off.

"If there are any," I say, almost to myself.

"They don't hand out calling cards like spies in movies," says Javier firmly. "They just pop up unpleasantly out of your day, *booff!* like a parking ticket or a flasher. Hands that are ludicrous can inflict as much unhappiness as dignified ones. If you want to sleep alone, sleep alone. And keep the car keys if it makes you feel better. No one here forces anyone to do anything."

He stands up and carefully brushes the sawdust from his shoulders and his jeans. He grips my shoulder. "You're a strong girl. You can take it. You can take this into your life. You might even be better for it, who knows." He bends down to kiss the back of my head and then he walks out the door.

I take the keys out of my pocket and throw them after him.

He moves up the hill to the trailer in the cool, intense sunlight. When he is ten steps away, the door opens and Luis appears. Then the door closes after both of them.

Slowly, the heavy calm of the house begins to fill in. I look around me. I'm alone in the place that, until now, the men have so studiously avoided bringing me to. I wonder what exactly it is that makes things different. I can't be sure.

"You can take this into your life."

It scares me, what I could take into my life. But whatever I can take, Javier can take more and still stay the same person. I want to know how. I know I'll stay here until I do. And he's aware of that. I can't tell if he's just sized me up, or if he thinks he'll help me grow into my power. Or if he has decided I would just grow into it myself, while the mountain buckles and nourishes and lightens and darkens around us.

The room we've slept in appears to be a small parlor. Near the floor and around the windows the plaster is coming away in strips. The iron window-grilles are rusted, and the broken window glass halos the room with squares and shards.

The wooden crates we felt our way around in the night are piled three or four high and deep around the mattress. They're labeled with letters and woven shut with chicken wire.

I look up at the trailer, but from outside the slatted, frosted windows give no clue to what is going on inside. I sit down and start to untwist the wire ends on the nearest case.

It takes a long time, and even once they're free of

each other the wires rotate in the air like thorns gone
haywire or grasping hands.

I retrieve my set of car keys, which landed on the
veranda. With them, the work goes twice as fast.

When I reach out to touch Javier, I can feel the dark
reaching back to me and I can feel my own glow rip-
ping through it.

Being with him, either I'll fall into that shadow once
and for all or I'll light it away.

I sit back on my heels.

It's about time.

When I was in high school, a stained glass studio in
Manhattan had offered advanced classes. So from nine
to twelve on Saturday mornings I learned how to carry
plate glass so it wouldn't shatter in my arms ("glass is
a reactive material," Mr. Schonberg said with a frown,
making it clear that if I hurt myself it would be no one's
fault but my own), and from one to five I spent in bed
with Adam.

He always opened the door to me with a proud-
bashful dip of the head, his newly broadened shoulders
hunching in as if to shield some inner essence. His was
an almost graceful awkwardness that both protected
him and beckoned me in. I would follow those shoulders around a corner, past a kitchen, through Mariah's
cheerful living room, and into the bedroom wing.

That shadowy, imperfect impression he always gave
elsewhere faded to almost nothing among the shadows
and bright colors of Mariah's apartment. But I was
choosing to see past it, and this secret generosity of mine
was intoxicating. We would sit on his white bed, listen

to James Taylor, and make love silently before we really spoke. The bedroom floor was dark gray. Charcoal shadows fell over us through the drawn blinds, and the pinked blue light of the large aquarium flickered over us as we held each other.

The first few weeks I was already pulled there by habit. It was strange, to know so little about my passion or him and yet show up punctually at his door week after week.

We never mentioned Elise or Mariah or Lars unless it was for a practical reason, usually to do with how one or the other of them was going to get one or the other of us from one place to another in an expedient way earlier or later in the day, thus allowing us to eke out more time with each other. But even so, they were there with us like the roots of some enormous creaking oak where we, the woodchucks, were nesting. Although we listened with trepidation to the trunk and branches creaking in the wind, without them we'd have been scrambling through the muck.

There was a scene in a trashy novel I'd read that often came back to me after we had made love and Adam had disappeared to make our lunch. In this book an enlightened teenaged heroine resolved to go to bed with her boyfriend. Like me and my friends, this heroine knew she would only consider her achievement (and it was an achievement) accomplished once she had enjoyed sex. As far as she was concerned, without the payoff, penetration itself was just another challenge which contained the potential for grievous and harmful error, like learning to drive or opening a checking account.

This absurd, uncanny anxiety of hers had struck a chord with me, along with the story's unlikely denouement: once this girl had set her cap for pleasure, both act and appreciation occurred at once, in a charming location, and seemingly without effort. As she lay waiting, her senses open, her mind curious and engraving each sensation into memory, first she felt pain, then a nondescript mechanical pressure, and then, as she phrased it, a pleasant sensation that built and then dropped off; one, two, three, like a troika of horsemen riding through her body on their way to some more urgent destination.

That was where I'd become unnerved. Because I was finding crossing the boundary between pain and pleasure to be more like a slow downshifting of gears on an almost endless hill. I was relentlessly in control. Each week things would be better. And I was sure we were easing away a nameless thing so another, wonderful thing could take its place. But there we were in the middle of it, Adam and I, trying our best to control the momentum of an ominous and sacred force in slow, careful, reverential steps.

It was hard to get him to say much. His only obvious passion was for the forces and creatures of the sea, but even on the one Saturday we'd spent at the aquarium, he'd met each of my questions with a smile and kneaded my back in answer instead. He refused to discuss his own fish with me except for the occasional aside about how you had to be very careful about which varieties you put together, because they might destroy each other. And after we made love he always stole away to make the lunches that fortified us for actual conversation, were well balanced, and which always came garnished with sprigs of parsley and radish flowers.

◊

I wished he'd mention Lars once in a while. Aside from that it was easy. When I was with him I felt like a fish moving through a fast black river. And when Schonberg gave us the assignment to do a river in stained glass, I wasn't surprised, it simply corroborated something I already knew.

The assignment began with a design, or cartoon, which he asked us to do during the week at home. First I broke my image down into pieces, looking for the deep structure inside so I could express it with the soldered lead that would hold together each piece of glass I chose and cut to fit my pattern. It was an interesting problem. It was like doing a jigsaw puzzle, but backwards: you didn't start with the frame's flat edges, you started with the center, and added each piece and color, radiating outwards, until you got to that edge. And, you were planning it on paper, so the color and light, which was the point, could only go on in your mind.

As I went along, I checked to make sure that the proportion of image to ground, in this case, the river to its bank, was not too large. And then came the fun part, where I got to think about the perfect setting for this window, and about what kind of light would come through the window there, and how the changing color effects of the landscape behind it would affect it. Then I got to plan the colors and kinds of glass that would harmonize best.

I was elated when Schonberg immediately approved my design cartoon on Saturday morning. After a brief lecture about choices in leading, which, he revealed, was the purpose behind the assignment of rendering water which has no predictable lines, I began to pick my final colors. I was the only one allowed to—everyone else had to revise—and I went at my task with gusto.

Some kinds of glass are perfectly clear; others rippled, bubbled, and streaked. Some have a single color; others are colored in layers. That day, I held each sheet up to bright daylight. And that was when the sheet of expensive green English streaky glass recoiled from my hands and shattered on the floor.

I wasn't hurt, just shaken at my own negligence, my own power to do wrong. The few seconds it took me to look down at the broken glass had seemed like minutes, and looking down at them was like looking over the edge of a cliff. But the sheet had broken pretty evenly: a little crumbling at the edges, no spurs at the sides. Those broken pieces struck me as so viscous, so shining, so substantial. Schonberg was always lecturing us about tapping first: if there was a crack in the sheet, we would hear a vibrating rattle. It was such an odd ritual, like something out of a fairy tale. But this sheet I had not tapped, but lifted, so sure and swift I was for my desire to make that particular current of green thread through the tributary I was constructing in my mind.

The fragments were my responsibility, something to tend: something alive. I had to find a way to fix my mistake. I realized they'd be a beautiful river if I soldered them together as they lay. I watched the soft green veins brush through the milky-clear ground of the large shards of streaky glass and then disappear in the momentum of other green veins, in other fragments, at every side. Flowing this way and that, they developed a direction. And I knew how to contain them.

Schonberg thought my plan worthless. He looked pointedly at my original cartoon, with its carefully balanced lead lines. This new river of mine would have no such balanced composition. But since I had to pay for the glass anyway, he had to relent. For the rest of the workshop, he ignored me. It was then that I recalled how he'd once mentioned a glass artist who'd dropped a sheet and been so inspired by the patterns it broke into that he leaded it together, then and there. Schonberg had been scornful of this artist, maintaining what he had done wasn't art, or even craft. But that just told me Schonberg's life was a different kind of life than the lives this artist and I had. Putting together the pieces the way chance had left them made perfect sense to me.

◇

The lunch Adam made us later that afternoon consisted of Croque-Messieurs stuffed with at least a half pound each of ham and cheese, adorned with a sprig of parsley and three cherry tomatoes and accompanied by a knife and fork and napkin tied together with a piece of bakery string.

For a few minutes, all of our attention was absorbed by the need to take neat and seemly bites out of the massive sandwiches.

"You used to be so quiet," Adam said then.

I was caught off guard. Usually we talked about nothing—movies, current events, whatever I happened to be doing in Schonberg's class. Besides, as far as I was concerned, he was the quiet one.

"And now what am I?" I asked, stretching slowly across the sheets. That made me feel better. I never dressed for lunch, I felt more protected naked, as if without my clothes I assumed a second, more potent identity. His eyes moved across me. He cast them downward and smiled as if to signal he had just logged crucial information.

"Pretty," he said. And repeated: "Pretty."

"You're much nicer now than you were then," I said. I paused and looked over at him. Something about the way he held his head reminded me of Lars that morning at home, storming around with his mouth set in a shaky line. It had been an unusual, more intimate view of the very formal man who was my stepfather than I was usually allowed. "Mom wouldn't like it if she knew about us," I added.

"Dad wouldn't care. It would be fine by Dad."

"How would you know? You never talk to him."

"Yes, I do."

I turned around.

"You do?" As far as I knew, Lars and Adam hadn't spoken in about a year, and spoken only sporadically in the two years before that. No one knew why, and I didn't dare ask for all the unhappiness it would stir up. At home, just mentioning his name made Lars's face tighten.

"I speak to him in my dreams."

Adam was sprawled on his stomach on the bed, staring at the floor. There was a self-satisfied expression on his face. I stood up and walked over to the aquarium.

"Dad's so weird," Adam remarked to himself.

That confused me. Aside from that night when Lars could have seen us together and this morning, I'd always found Adam's father remarkably collected; even subdued. Glancing back over at Adam, I decided it was best not to pursue.

The air in the room was getting thinner. I thought again about Lars's behavior, and how, coming from him, it almost smacked of emergency. This was just the newest of the many pieces of information I possessed about his father that Adam did not. I toyed with the idea of mentioning it to him and then rejected it. I might be mistaken, and I didn't want to stir up more trouble. Once was enough for today.

Now Adam came up behind me and buried his hands under my arms as though he were burying them in an old and favorite pair of gloves. He moved his palms comfortably down my body and rested them lightly over my hipbones.

"I'd never been with a girl before you," he whispered.

I tilted my head and closed my eyes.

He reached between my legs and opened me with his thumbs and carefully pushed me to my knees. I'd spied a small collection of pornography poking out from the corner of the bedspread, and this must have been the result. I reached out to him, out to that smooth, firm hip almost as pleasingly vulnerable as my own, and we moved together, and soon, very quietly and easily, he entered me from behind. I felt a tremor of surprise run through him as if he couldn't quite believe he'd pulled off this particular feat.

I opened my eyes, which I'd shut against him as he entered me, and found myself regarding our reflected faces in the glass of the tank. His eyes were still closed. Adam's hair covered half his face and his partially open mouth was nursing air from a space between my shoulder and my ear. The burble of the water pump added a lushness to the scratchy, lean rhythms of our breath. And Adam's striped and bowed tetras floated in and out of his open mouth and across my collarbone and shoulder blades. Other, longer and more subtly colored fish hovered in the back corners, watching us. I let my eyes drift until the tank was a moving field of color, and arched up to meet Adam's deep stroke. Relieved by the reprieve from our conversation, I gave myself up to the color and rhythm.

Then something new happened. I began to experience an almost intellectual satisfaction from the successful mechanics of what we were doing, one akin to that small yet comforting pleasure one feels when sud-

denly a recalcitrant key turns easily and smoothly in a
lock; proof certain things can be orderly and reliable in
a disorderly and unpredictable world. No ecstasy, no
epiphany, or loss of control. Just relief, curiosity, and a
feeling of usefulness. Above all, a feeling of usefulness.
I began to arch and rock and angle against him in search
of the slightest hint of pleasure. Our excitement at this
new achievement made us rise slightly, and my breasts
brushed against the cold aquarium. Again I looked into
it and this time I caught Adam watching me. Our eyes
met, his as veiled and cold as fish eyes. For the first
time, I saw in them the intimation of natural advantage
that had dominated their expression when we lived together as brother and sister. He gently moved me back
a few inches, scooped my left breast into his hand, and
rolled my nipple between two fingers as we watched
ourselves and each other in the glass. His movements
deepened and gained urgency. The look of superiority
was replaced with one of supplication. Now I was staring him down, and the painful *thing* was all but abol-
ished, all but replaced with an almost Calvinistic
determination to perform a task well. As he lowered
me to the floor I began to feel something else, a faint,
deep, physical purring. The carpet pile warmed us, in-
vigorated us, I breathed in the last traces of the soap
Mariah'd used on it and that smell twisted around and
around with the less and less tentative thrumming inside me. There was an interior current we had to follow, a sort of underground spring. Adam's hands were
everywhere, kneading, stroking, grasping until his limbs
tensed and extended like a diver's and far away I could
hear a phone ringing and ringing.

    The phone stopped. He pulled out of me, turned me
to him, and kissed my mouth. The phone started again.

He ran to answer it.

I looked up and saw the fish swimming through the reflection of my slick body. Slowly, slowly the purring subsided. Even the subsiding was pleasant. I ran my hand over my body.

"Okay," I heard Adam saying. "I don't know. Okay." Silence. "Uh huh. No. No." Tapping. "No. Eight o'clock."

I heard his footsteps walking away. About five minutes later, his footsteps walked back. I couldn't move. I felt like a prisoner. My head was heavy, my limbs were heavy.

Adam was fully dressed.

He sat on the bed and began to pull his sneakers over clean white socks.

"Who was that?" I pulled over his robe and wrapped myself in it.

"My father."

I sat up. Too many things were going on at once.

"There's something wrong with Lars?" I said out loud.

"No. No. He wants to have dinner. Dinner!" Adam thew his hands up in the air in an uncharacteristically flamboyant gesture.

"Adam." I sat up and looked into his face. "We just had lunch."

"I told him. He's coming here."

"Here," I said.

"He was in a pay phone." Adam finished tying the second sneaker and stood up. He blinked. "I don't know why. I tried to tell him."

"Adam," I said. I remembered how Lars had looked that morning, and wondered if it bore any relation to this phone call. I drew the robe even more tightly

around me. He couldn't come here. This place was a safe place, and once he came here it would be just like anywhere else.

"No time anyway for you to leave," Adam said sadly. I looked at him closely. He seemed different. There was some new detail about him that was embarrassing, that I should avert my eyes from for his sake, but I couldn't figure out what it was exactly. His face was grayed, and he didn't know what to do with his hands. Then I saw it. Adam's mouth was set in that same thin line of worry.

"I'm staying right here," I said.

"He might come in here."

I was angry. "Then where should I go?"

"Mom's room." He had picked up one of the porn magazines and was flipping through it. His voice was exaggeratedly light. "He won't go there."

I stood up and collected my clothes.

"He didn't say anything about coming to the city today," I said. "He said he wasn't feeling well and was going to do some paperwork."

Adam's face flooded with pain. Then his eyes lit on where the terry cloth came apart at the top of my robe. He pulled it open and squeezed one of my breasts. The look of anguish blanched out of him.

"C'mon," he said, keeping the hand in my robe as he guided me out of his bedroom and into Mariah's. I took in a gold-flocked bedspread and walls covered with tasseled hangings. Adam locked the door behind us. He opened my robe, pushed my legs apart, and stroked me. The doorbell rang. He bounded out the door.

I locked it behind him and looked around. There was a picture of him and John as toddlers on the bedside table, and a framed quote from the Bhagavad in calligraphy. The mahogany mirror over the dresser overpowered dark jars with their own handwritten labels. *Patchouli. Musk. Raspberry.* I picked one up and tilted it and a dark oil stretched up the sides. I thought of my mother's bureau, laden with glass bottles finished off with shiny paper labels and French words, the palest of gold liquids trembling inside them. One day, as I browsed through them, she'd dived toward me and sealed up a bottle whose heavy beveled top I had been examining in one hand. "You have to be careful," she'd said, "they evaporate." Then she took out the stopper again, quickly dabbed it behind each of my ears, and looked at me knowingly.

Now I rubbed a little of the dark oil on my pulse points, got dressed, and sat straight up on the bed with my feet tucked under me as though I were sitting on a bus. I had the irrational feeling there was something very potent and perhaps dangerous under the golden, pillowy expanse and that if I lay down I would be at risk.

The low, even-metered flow of Lars's voice soaked through the walls. I caught a few words: *must, mean.* Adam's voice surfaced now and then in short, subdued bursts. I remember thinking Lars was speaking with great ease for a man who hadn't talked to his son in a year. In fact, I'd never heard Lars hold forth so fluently and expansively with anyone, not even my mother. He was one of those men who thought saying something more than once was a form of capitulation.

I thought of how Lars's face always looked during breakfast the days he took John to see his mother. His chin would pull in defensively and he'd blink repeatedly, as if he had a headache. John, who'd developed a sensitive, hollowed, soulful look soon after he came back from two years with Mariah, would sit blankly at the table, like a commuter at a bus station, until his father rumbled, "Okay," and paced out to the car, pulling John along behind him as if magnetically. More often than not, my mother did not attend these breakfasts. Once, on my way downstairs, I caught her sorting all her jewelry, which was strewn over the bed, quietly humming Cole Porter songs. Lars usually didn't come back from these trips until late afternoon, and on those evenings they often went out for dinner alone. "Hippie," I heard him say once, doubtfully, as he stopped on the flagstone path to clean his glasses as they left for the restaurant. In response my mother trilled that wonderful, bell-like laugh of hers that loved and discredited and threw everything to the four winds all at the same time. Then she hooked her arm through his, and led him firmly to the car.

Now Lars's vigorous baritone dropped down to a gruff rumble. "Yeah," I heard Adam say. In comparison his voice was tight, closed off. "Yeah, okay." Chairs pushed back, and their voices moved off toward the door. I breathed a sigh of relief. Then the voices—now offhand and easy, like the voices of two men who do business together often and almost trust each other—traveled back toward me. I held my breath. They passed by Mariah's room toward Adam's. "Figure a few months," Lars was saying. Then their voices were smoothed over by the burble of the water pump. I wondered if Lars'd be able to sense our wake. Ten minutes later, I heard them amble toward the front of the apartment again. "The jackfish can't really live in captivity unless they're very young," Adam was saying, as if in agreement with himself. Irrationally, I told myself, it hurt me that he'd talk about his fish with his father but not with me.

More scraping of chairs, and the voices stopped. A door closed. I heard someone, Lars, I was almost sure, blow his nose. The page of a newspaper turned. A spoon or fork clinked against glass or china. This went on. Had Adam left me alone with Lars? It seemed impossible. Still, I couldn't hear him anymore. I told myself to be patient and still and all this would be over and I wouldn't have to expend any extra energy over it. Adam and I were so close to taming that pain, that force, that *thing* we were drawn to; we were moving so surely and swiftly now down that hill, through that current; soon we would be borne out on the vast, salt-pure sea and all the darkness, the narrowness, the hidden turbulence would be smoothed away. We'd laugh as we rocked on the waves and sailed away from the house on the hill, the shadowy apartment, the bottles of oil and perfume, the glaze we carried around us which had become trivial, far behind us. He would know then as I always had, that we could not be together forever, but that we would always share that triumph, a triumph no one else could ever appreciate. I needed that victory the way I needed to nurture the purring inside me.

After a few more minutes of scrapes and harrumphs, whoever was at the table stood up and began to walk around; a few steps this way, then in the other direction. The refrigerator opened, then closed. With a sinking feeling, I realized it had to be Lars doing an inventory of sorts. The logical finale of such an inventory did not escape me. I was glad I'd locked the door.

He moved off toward the living room and I heard the air conditioner hum louder, then still louder, and settle back to medium. The steps moved back through the kitchen and stopped in front of my door. The handle turned. It turned the other way.

"Mariah?" said Lars's voice, strangely thin and rough at the same time. I looked down at my hands.

"Mar, are you napping?" He emphasized the word incredulously. Silence. "Oh." This more contritely, the delicacy of the situation finally sinking in. "I just need to check in with you about something. Didn't mean to barge in. Didn't know you were here. Mar?"

I drew myself into a ball, thinking of Schonberg's class and tracing patterns over the new sheet of green streaky with my pencil.

"Mariah." He said it very loudly and clearly, as if speaking to an intelligent but lazy child. "I needed to see our son. Don't worry, I didn't tell him exactly. First I wanted to talk to you."

I willed him not to push the door in and find me there. I felt flimsy. I listened to his powerful male breathing outside the door for a few more minutes and then, mercifully, he moved down the hall to Adam's room.

I turned and looked at the books on the little shelf next to Mariah's bed: *The Little Prince, The Prophet, On Becoming a Person,* a biography of Martha Graham, *A Spy in the House of Love.* A miniature reproduction of a Degas dancer neatly halved the empty space at the end of the shelf. I studied the books and the dancer for a long time. They were something else, they had nothing to do with all this, and while I looked at them neither did I.

I opened the door, closed it behind me, and walked into Adam's room.

Lars was staring at the aquarium and tapping the glass. He didn't notice me come in. Most of the fish were frightened, hanging in the back, but then one came up to him and nursed the glass where his finger was touching.

"That's the way," Lars crooned. "Pretty thing."

"It's me," I said loudly.

Lars turned around. First he looked shocked, then his face softened.

"Why, Vanessa," he said, as if I were interchangeable with any other child who had become part of this family for one reason or another, and therefore logically belonged there with him. "I didn't hear you come in."

I was saved. "I guess I'm pretty quiet. You know."

"Yeah," he said, "you are." His blue eyes were blurred and kindly, which was how they got when he drank wine at dinner. "Come here," he said, and gestured with one arm.

Astonished, I complied.

"Your brother went out to get us some milk," he said. "There wasn't any milk for coffee. I guess he ran into a long line, or maybe he's up to something."

I nodded.

"Your brother told me the names of all these critters," Lars said. "The full names in Latin." This, he enunciated clearly and proudly. "Know what they are?"

I shook my head. There was a stain on the rug that was making me uncomfortable, but Lars didn't seem to have noticed it. The room smelled of sex. My mother would have noticed it. Mariah would have noticed it. Even my father would have noticed it. But all of that seemed like a dream. Lars's presence had squeezed all the life out of our life-giving secret and pushed it back into the place of dreams.

"Here," he said. "This is a *chaetoderma penicilligera*. This, I am given to understand, is the *chaetodon collare*. And this is a *hyphessobrycon scholzei*." He took some special pleasure out of repeating those names. "Can you imagine that? And you can't put certain ones in a tank together. For instance, there is something called a yellow-tailed anemone fish. It seems you can't put a yellow-tailed anemone fish in a tank with anything but another sort of anemone fish. I believe there is a clown variety, for instance. And add some sea anemone flowers or else, he told me." Lars imitated Adam's voice. "Something, huh? Or else what?" He turned and looked at me as if I held the answer. "Complicated. Your brother told me he doesn't tell anyone their names, not even his girlfriend. He says they eat a lot less than his girlfriend. I told him, nothing surprising about that. Weird. Old Adam's getting weird on us, like his mom. Not telling the names of his fish to his girlfriend." He looked at me sideways. "I didn't know he had a girlfriend. Did you know he had a girlfriend?"

"No," I said.

I gathered my things and walked out the door. My heart was pounding.

Walking down the street I felt wiped clean, fresh, blank.

◇

On the train home I tried to come up with explanations for being at Adam's but I was exhausted by all the clearness and sought pleasure watching the sun set on the summer-black Hudson instead.

As it turned out no one asked.

When I got there, Adam was sitting on our front porch. In his eyes I saw the exhaustion and clarity I felt. He looked past me and through me, rubbing one pale knee.

And instead of being angry with him I felt chastised. All the questions were bleached out of me.

I went through the screen door, and there was Elise in the kitchen, in white Bermuda shorts and a flowered T-shirt, sealing sandwich halves into little plastic bags and cradling the telephone receiver between her ear and shoulder with her back to me.

"It seems he found Adam at home and told him about his illness." Her hands were flying across the counter. "He must have been so mixed up and excited, at least he got that part right. And then the poor boy went out to get milk for coffee but he was so badly shaken by what he'd heard he ended up hitchhiking here. You know they hadn't spoken for a long time. I still don't think he knows what hit him."

She didn't see me. Her eyes were unusually velvety and she was blinking rapidly.

"No. Lars couldn't help himself. Not once he'd stopped taking the medication long enough. There's just so long . . . Well, yes, he'd stop when he felt the energy surge coming along, because he could take advantage of it if he had a major report to deliver. It's not that uncommon. But there's just so long . . . Well yes, there's still always some logic or other to what happens next, yes. That's called episodes. But while he was waiting for Adam his mood shifted . . . or he might have felt both ways at the same time, we don't know, that's called a mixed state . . ." Elise's voice faded away, then came back briskly. "And Adam didn't come back. Adam came here. And Mariah is touring. So eventually the neighbors smelled the gas from the oven and called the super and he opened the door and found him and then they called. But it was over then. Just over." Elise was finished with the sandwiches. She put her hand to the telephone receiver, turned her head, and saw me.

Sit down, she mouthed. "Eleanor, I have to go. Vanessa's here."

I just stood there, my tongue and thoughts bulked in cotton.

Seeing my distress, Elise took my hands and we sat down together. Then she told me.

Lars had a condition called manic depression. They'd discovered it a year or two after she'd married him, although he'd probably had it before she met him but no one had known he was sick. He and she had planned to tell us about it, except the medicine had worked so well they didn't feel we would notice anything, and he had been so concerned about what we would think of him and how it would affect us.

I nodded mutely.

She patted her fuzzy brown topknot several times more than was necessary, looked out the window and at her watch, stood up, carried her pile of sandwiches and bags from the counter to the table, sat down, and set back to work.

While she explained to me that there were times when Lars stopped taking his lithium, which was the medication that controlled the symptoms, or decreased the dosage without telling anyone, she started blinking again. At first when he hadn't taken it he wouldn't say anything or do anything unusual, but eventually he'd say he was going to work and disappear. Elise explained she couldn't tell he hadn't been taking it until he had an episode, and by then it was too late. She looked out the window.

"Once I had to go pick him up in Atlanta. He'd taken a plane and checked into a hotel. He was convinced his company should immediately set up a branch office there. He must have stopped taking the medication again recently. You know, the doctors tell you not to second-guess when you think there's trouble, because it can make them insecure." She squeezed her eyes shut and opened them again, and when she did they were brighter. "He'd planned to go into the office over this weekend, but I guess somewhere along the line he got it in his head to go tell Adam about his condition. When I called his office they said he'd left, and something about going to the city, so I started making calls. I tried Mariah's, but no one answered. I hoped he'd ended up at a museum or something, or that he'd gone to meet you at class, and then he'd call me."

She looked straight at me now and when she spoke again her voice was very level. "But Lars didn't call," she said quietly. "And Lars died. Now the Apfels are coming to drive us into the city. You heard. I'm getting ready. I'm glad you're here, darling. We didn't know where to find you."

There was a little place inside me, a kind of air pocket, like the protective hollow our parents made for me and Adam, except this was a place I made for myself. I was sinking into it, and away.

"Are you going like that?" I was looking at her white shorts.

She looked at me indulgently.

"What does it matter how I go?" she said.

The tangled chicken wire at Los Anenomes finally begins to make sense. I ease each wire free from its mate and lift the top off the crate.

Inside are four rows of six fifths of bar-brand vodka. I open two more boxes in different areas of the room.

More vodka.

Outside, the sun is icing the trailer with light. The unlit windows have darkened like hollow eyes with the daylight, and a pot of coffee is simmering on the camp stove.

I look for any sign: a sleeve in a window, the shudder

of a door, the stretching and distortion of light behind darkness that means a window is opening behind a fine screen. The coffee froths down the side of the pot and still there is no one.

I sit back on my heels and imagine all the quiet rooms beyond the one I'm in, rooms where other women came to remove themselves from time when Los Anenomes was a sanitarium.

The sun pours in on my face and shoulders. I'm still tired. I notice my upper arms are flicked with faint, finger-sized purple marks. The room I'm in smells of must and sunlight and fresh whitewash. Outside, the coffee is still boiling quietly.

I stand up and make my way across a thin strip of open floor to the inner door. It pries open rather easily and leads to the broken-tiled threshold of a dark public room. Probably it once had been a ballroom, and later, perhaps a dining room for the women. A large black fireplace dominates the north wall, and the south wall is lined with dark windows that face an inner court-yard. I can make out the swooping, shiplike lines of a grand piano near the back. The room has been swept clean, and neat stacks of firewood are drying in one corner.

A bright hallway leads off to the left. I run lightly through it past the broken windows, hoping I won't be seen, and up into a wider, airier corridor of bedrooms. The outer rooms face south toward the hill; through the windows of the inner rooms I see a small courtyard with a white stone fountain.

I think of the nuns moving silently through the halls, their arms full of clean linen, their eyes focused dis-creetly to one side.

I look into the inner bedrooms, the empty ones. But

these are the faded, secretive uncommunicative surfaces of women who respected the property of others. Women who would have considered leaving their mark a sign of bad upbringing. Women who knew how to move house.

I guess at least in that last respect they were women like me.

The outer rooms are filled with crates stacked three high.

One room is filled with crates of Scotch, a second with crates of white rum, and the third with gin.

That hall ends in another staircase, and the bedrooms on the next floor are smaller and tidier. The first room contains, as the caption informs me, a print of Saint Isabel of Portugal, in Coimbra after she gave up the Queen's throne. A tall woman throws a golden shower of alms to the poor from her window while the sea glows lavender behind her, a trick of age and light.

The next six rooms are filled with crates of Scotch, each with a number penciled neatly in chalk on the bottom right-hand corner of the door.

The last room is the whitewashed one. A faded dhurrie lines up neatly with a foam mattress, and a blue sleeping bag is folded at one end of the mattress. A small wood table and chair is positioned under the window, and the wardrobe on a third wall is padlocked shut. A box of matches is neatly balanced on top of the small butane heater to one side. On the wall above the mattress someone has written with a burnt match:

Maite   Maite   Maite

Taped to the wardrobe's bottom right corner is a photograph of Javier with both his arms clasped around the girl whose picture I'd seen in the apartment and again in the car. In the picture Javier is wearing a hat. Under that hat his eyes lock on the camera lens in his usual reflex of assessment, but his mouth smiles. One of the girl's hands touches the arm that holds her as if to ease him. Her lips are slightly parted and she gazes squarely into the camera.

I look out the window. The hill here falls away so quickly that this room actually sits quite high in the air. Inside, the room feels larger, and it seems peaceful. Outside, I can see the tops of pine trees, another hill rising to the south, and, between them, a bit of the road that goes toward town.

This is the room where I would have chosen to stay, too.

But it's taken.

Before I can do too much thinking, I move on.

I begin to feel uncomfortable. The house doesn't add up. Why would Javier's bar be so overstocked that he has to store the overflow here, miles and miles from town? And most of the cartons stored on this second floor, while the cavernous common room lies empty? I follow a rotting staircase back to the first floor and wander through arches that connect three small, white, decaying parlors at the front of the house. At the back of the third parlor I find a yellow door.

It leads down into a room that still holds two long wooden tables, a stack of easels, two ceramic stands, and what looks like an old fire-burning kiln.

Luis is standing on the far side of the kiln.

"I saw you through the windows," he says.

He looks so calm and so young, like an orderly or a saint.

"You and I should talk," says Luis.

CHAPTER TEN

◇

I sit on a shellacked bench made from half a log at one of the long tables. The wood is faded and porous like wood that has been left out in the rain. It's definitely an older kiln I see. I've seen pictures of kilns like this in books.

Luis sits across from me. He bows his head and looks up at me shyly. I see he's one of those people who rein themselves in to become invisible in company and let themselves out when they're alone. Right now, he's holding himself somewhere way above this room, above this encounter with me. But he's also entirely here.

"You care about my brother-in-law," he says.

"What was wrong with the kiln?"

"We couldn't channel the heat." He nods at the burn marks. "We almost burned the house down. And there wasn't a chimney, either. It was closed up a long time ago." He examines me closely. "Believe me, I'm as sorry as you are. I wanted turkey for Christmas."

I look at the kiln. "We could do something with the windows. This house could have very beautiful windows again."

Luis shrugs. The edge of a knee, covered with golden down, protrudes from a rip in his jeans. I think he means for me to see it, but the exhibition is certainly as much for his pleasure as for mine.

"Maybe you will be here to appreciate them." He puts a cigarette in his mouth, leans forward, and lights it with more matches from Javier's restaurant. "Listen carefully," he continues, "because I can only bear to tell you once. And our friend must know nothing of our conversation." His soft brown eyes rest briefly on the faint marks on my neck and arms then wander back to the table.

"We are here because of that problem with Danny. But it is not the problem that you think it is. As you know, your friend is reentering the world of politics. He is contributing heavily to one group that is helping an overthrow of the military government. He hopes to join them when the moment is right. But a lot of his money is tied up at home and the value is just wearing away with that shit of an economy. So a good percentage of his financial contribution is coming from product he sells off in North Africa."

"Danny's boat. You're not telling me you guys are honest-to-gosh rumrunners."

"Right now, rum, as you call it, yes. Sometimes other things. It depends. But Danny. Danny was supposed to be making a delivery. But instead he left *Planetario* in Tangier and took the ferry to Cadiz with a friend and a quarter key of hash. Hash, we don't know why.

Drugs, we avoid. He was picked up in customs, easy. Stupid." Luis almost spits this last word. I can see he prides himself on being able to hold his own like a much older man. "Javier was pretty shook up. Then our customer told us the shipment never arrived. So we do not know if it is still on its way, lost en route, or confiscated with the boat. Of course, if it was confiscated and is traced back to Javier, he will be deported. And he has nowhere to be deported to. So we're stuck here with our pants down and this big order waiting to go out."

"So Javier has nowhere to be deported but back there again."

Luis nods. "Possibly. That's what he thinks anyway. Sometimes, though, I suspect it is wishful thinking on his part. Sometimes, I think he thinks it would be a relief just to get it over with."

"And here they won't find him."

"Well, he thinks it's less likely, anyway. Sometimes he does not show the best of self-preservation instincts. Here they might not find him. I guess."

I'm standing up then, and walking around the room. That begins to explain why he was so worried about his passport.

Luis watches me tranquilly, and begins to blow a chain of easy, perfect smoke rings like a basketball player winding down with a string of dunk shots.

"He should have taken you home when he found you. I'm sorry. I couldn't believe my eyes when I saw the two of you just drinking coffee in broad daylight as if you were sitting on the Champs-Élysées."

"You mean you two had a plan to meet here?"

"Yes. Later. To stay quietly until things worked themselves out. Why he took off early with you . . ." A sad smile finishes the sentence.

"So why are you here?"

Luis shrugs. "My life got tangled up with his years ago. I had nowhere else to go. We share certain things, a certain past. Because of them, we need each other. It is time for me to move on now. It is better for us both. But I would prefer to leave on good terms, to have matters provided for."

"Of course," I say carefully, "it sounds like you're skipping out just when things are getting rough."

He drops the cigarette stub on the floor and grinds it out. "You think this is rough?"

Luis stands up and walks me over to the kiln. He pulls it away from the wall and kneels down. "The heat has to be channeled this way, I think." He points to a black pipe near the base of the oven. "It needs some kind of hook piece to suck it through."

Outside, the wind is rising. Azaleas are bobbing in and out of the window edges, and down the road I can see the white Fiat moving slowly up the hill. Javier is driving.

I kneel next to Luis and peer at the blackened metal-wood tray and the pipes threading through the kiln opening. Luis is easy to be next to. He rests his left hand on the small of my back. That's easy, too.

"See?" he says, moving his right hand back and forth in the empty space between the two pieces. "The problem is here. All these pipes were scattered on the floor. I got this far, and then there wasn't any more."

He smells faintly of sandalwood and lavender, and, close up, I see his cheeks are very smooth. This is a surprise, after the hard words.

We kneel there silently for a few seconds, gazing at the stove for no good reason.

"It can't be that difficult," I say, finally. "This was therapy for invalids, not a professional workshop."

He looks at me curiously. "What would you do to those windows?"

"I can't erase the cracks. But there are things you can do with paint or enamel. You can forget about a lot of processes without good equipment and supplies, but you can also be creative. I mean, think about what they used to do in Venice."

"You're funny," he says. "You're a little bossy, and you're a little naive. Yet any other woman but my sister probably would have been gone by now. You make a big effort."

I sit on the floor and lean back against the wall.

"I don't really understand you," I say.

He picks up my hand and holds it. "Maybe I can try to fix this oven," he says.

"Javier can take care of himself," I say.

"Not really. He can't stand to be alone," says Luis. He stands up and holds his hands out to me. I take them, and he pulls me to my feet. "So will you stay here with him? You'd be good at it. You could really handle him. And you're American—you'd be safe." Then he looks at me and rolls his eyes, bringing me in on the joke contained in his last statement. Except I'm not sure which joke it is. "You could do it," he says. He gives me the sort of soft, confident look friends give each other.

"No, I couldn't. I mean, I don't think so."

"Not a word of this," says Luis.

◊

As we round the far side of the house I see a white stone gazebo pushing up against the woods. I can't take my eyes off the way the sun plays over the semitranslucent dome. I lose myself in its movement as highlights play over the dark, regular veins of color that show through from inside like a microscope lens probing an embryo.

Luis walks easily, almost jauntily. With one tight fist showing through the pockets of his windbreaker, he's like any boy walking his dog through a park on a blustery day. He puts one hand on the small of my back to guide me past a rock. I've left my jacket behind somewhere, but I'm not at all cold. My mind and body prickle with possibilities.

"It's odd," I say out loud. "A gazebo would belong with the fountain in back of the building. I suppose they were separated by the new wing."

"Do you want to go inside?" He knocks a piece of earth toward the gazebo with his foot. Neither of us mention the pile of whitened bones that cascade down the house's flank. No skulls: I check. But I do notice how white and smooth the bones are, and how looking at them really is not that different from looking at a curious tree stump or an abandoned bird's nest. No beauty or horror, not right here.

"What's in it?" I ask.

"Don't know. Never been."

"Nah, don't believe it for a minute."

"Believe it."

I slip through the narrow doorway between two columns and he follows. The circular interior is small and faintly claustrophobic and smells of mildew. The darkness is shot through with suggestions of muted color; hallucinations of red and blue and green. A marble bench runs around the circumference. But before I can lift my eyes to the ceiling I detect a smell that's out of place, the sulphurous odor of a freshly struck match. And then I see the small light burning almost behind me.

Javier.

A stripe of blue light falls diagonally across the left half of his face. The rest of him is hidden in shadows. And I can feel the darkness gathering in him again.

He goes on smoking. The hand that holds the cigarette moves in and out of the light from the doorway and I try, without success, to remember how that hand held me.

"You almost scared me to death." I get out. Behind me I can hear Luis kicking at the loose tiles in the floor.

"Same here." Even though I can't see his face clearly, I can almost feel the rapid, skeptical glance. He goes dark on me so quickly, he dares me to call him back to his clarity. "I was going to come and find you," he continues. He pushes his hand into the air and then draws it back hesitantly, as if he hasn't decided which one of us it belongs to. "You'd been gone a long time."

"You, too."

My eyes are adjusting to the darkness. I wish I could tell how much of this melodrama is him, and how much is his language talking. Javier raises his eyebrows, and his face closes up under the blue slash that wanders across his cheek as he turns toward me.

"I come here often. I think and I rest."

And then I look up, and catch my breath. The roof is entirely made of stained glass. Green vines climb up the four compass points of the roof, deep-red peonies describe garlands in the interstices of space, and pale-yellow satin bows hover in the border between glass and stone. The whole mass is stitched together in a honeycomb of leaded panes, with a lighter web of metal foil running through.

I sit down on the bench opposite Javier.

"I've seen the house. The little sitting rooms, the big hall, the bedrooms upstairs. The occupied bedrooms."

He is immobile except for the bobbing cigarette light.

He dismisses my statement with a minor shrug of annoyance. I'm getting angry now, too. Why was he so careful to keep me in the dark before, so careful the subject provoked an argument, if he planned to let me roam through the house and find out for myself, and then pretend my discovery was unimportant?

"You gave the tour?" he asks Luis, not unpleasantly.

"No." He looks down at his feet. "I found her in the room with the oven."

"I'd love to try my hand at the windows." I lean forward and touch Javier's knee. "I could, if we could make the kiln work again."

Javier looks at me incredulously.

Luis turns his head to Javier, who stubs out his cigarette on the marble bench and nods. Luis bows his head and leaves quietly.

"*Flaco*," calls Javier.

"Yes?"

"Why don't you wait for us? We won't be long."

"Well. Fine."

Javier leans forward and looks at me closely.

Everything feels wrong.

"I come here," Javier begins, "to think, because aside from the very considerable charm and quality of this gazebo I find that when I am inside it everything outside ceases to exist. We used to have a *pasada* like this in Córdoba."

We eye each other in the half-light through the pools of color the roof throws on the walls and floor.

"I would have shown you the stockrooms myself," he says.

"When?"

"When the time was right."

"What's wrong?"

"Why didn't you ask me? Why did you ask him?"

"I didn't ask him," I say. "He was there, waiting."

"I was waiting for you, too. In the trailer. I didn't think you would stay in that house."

Is this the reason for his abrupt change in mood? I pause, taking this in.

"Why? Why should I have come? Did you ask me? You left me alone there." Just then I comprehend an essential difference between him and me. "Javier, do you remember what it's like to be curious?"

The eyes brighten, then recede. "Maybe the problem isn't quite clear." Suddenly, there is more sadness and reserve etched in his face.

"I don't even know what to say to you. You leave too much out." The cold in the stone is getting under my skin.

"Not important things."

"I have to take care of myself." I sound defensive. For the first time, I wish he spoke English.

"Of course. But for the moment, I seem to be taking better care of you than anyone. That's what you were just thinking, isn't it."

I don't reply.

"I see I'm correct," he says softly. "Well. That makes me happy. You're not easy."

"I'm trying to find a balance."

"Do you feel a balance when we are together?"

"Yes." It's slipped out of me in spite of myself.

"Yes," Javier says.

CHAPTER ELEVEN

"In the mountains everyone took turns patrolling. Javier, and my sister and the rest. Only I was exempt, and that was probably my sister's doing. Maite. She had those big liquid reproving eyes. Like chocolates. She had a little of the Madonna about her, you know? Even though she'd kill me for saying that. She had those firm rounded arms, and this strong chin. And I bet she went right up to him and said, '*Che,* he's too young to die for the people on some swampy hill just because his sister fell in love with a big Hero. Let him cook, or mind the radio.' Maite loved to talk tough.

"Now our Javier, he probably didn't need much convincing. Maybe there was another skinny little kid or two like me. But he looked real shook up the day I showed up, and for the first week or so whenever he talked to me he got real fidgety, like he had a loose piece clanging around inside.

"Everyone knew they had to patrol because the men who went to Cuba taught them. Also, they read about it in books. They imagined this austere Bolívar and his lean bunch marching through the bleak heights of the Cordillera to ambush the fat cats stuck in the glittering crevices of New Granada. And they remembered Che with his little date book in the Bolivian forest, writing down his kids' birthdays. No one read on the hill, but they all remembered."

Luis is standing against the wall. Sometimes he looks at me; sometimes his eyes go somewhere else. He's waiting for me to finish, and while he waits he talks. "Cooking suited me fine. And I used to listen carefully when the patrols came in for soup and whiskey, when there was some. You see, I became very fascinated by this seemingly pointless ritual activity from which I alone had been banned, and I eavesdropped. God, they went at it with gusto! It was all very abstract, and I don't know if it had any practical purpose. But they were like pigs scenting truffles, they craved pursuit, and betrayal. It was almost a sexual kind of thing, you know? They'd poke around for hours on the slopes looking for broken brush, for cigarette butts that they picked up and burned back to life; looking for anything a pursuer might have tossed away. And someone—the police—did leave things. Maybe they didn't come around as much or as close as Javier thought they did. Maybe it was somebody else some of the time. But the oddest things were left on the ground in the middle of nowhere: empty sugar packets, rubbers blown up like balloons; Maite once told me she saw a string of rosary beads wrapped around a jacaranda branch. The patrols were convinced a good part of this stuff had been left behind by the hunters to taunt them."

Luis stops.

The cyan pigment just coats the bottom of the bowl. Undissolved flecks of ground glass and pigment float through the liquid, particles of life in a small, dying sea. Luis is helping me seal shut the cracks in windows in the three small parlors in the front of Los Anenomes. We have so much free time at Los Anenomes, at least Luis and I do, that we devote hours to it.

I've spent a full week experimenting, being patient, watching the blue enamel run down the network of cracks like dye through the veins of a leaf, coating and celebrating every flaw and crevice like a lover. Then Luis comes by with the butane lamp and passes the flame over the lines of the pattern until they fuse into a well-fed, oleaginous shine. Butane is clumsy for glass; not enough air to the mix. And it took a week to get a consistency that would cover the window cracks but smooth them down, too. But I am patient.

When each window is done, Luis stands back with me and admires them.

"Holding together the sky," he said the first time, almost ruefully.

When we're done, we reach through the window and pull the outside shutters closed so no one outside will see our work.

◇

At Javier's suggestion, he and I have begun sleeping in the trailer with Luis. This happened right after our conversation in the gazebo. Javier and I haven't really discussed this, but I'm grateful to him for it. I need time. When Luis offered to sleep outside, I thanked him and declined. It's reassuring to hear his light breathing so close to mine; it makes me feel like I have a guardian, a way out. There are moments when I wonder why we sleep in a big silver trailer if Javier wants to avoid detection, but then it always slips my mind.

It was a few days after I settled in that I got tired of cooking and listening to the men argue about old times. That was when I walked into Los Anenomes and took careful stock of what was there.

Without a kiln or electricity for solder, I didn't know what came next exactly. But I had heard of things I could try. We did have the gas flame butane and a few of the rooms were littered with cake-glass in jewel tones I could grind down to powder. So I asked Luis to get a few items in town and he and I started experimenting. It took time to make a mixture we could liquefy with the gas flame, so we had been working together more than a few days when he started to tell me about the mountain.

"Javier was different then," Luis says now.

We both watch a rivulet of green go sugar-hard on the glass. It crosses the faraway road diagonally, so the two lines, near and far, target a point in midair.

When the glass line is completely still, Luis adds, "He suffered then. You could see it in his face. You could see it in his shoulders. He suffered for flesh-and-blood individuals. He felt responsible. These days, his *mala leche* is nonspecific. He simply wants to restore the entire world to its proper alignment, kind of a chiropractor or something."

"How old are you?" I ask. "Nineteen, twenty?"

He gives me a look that is half imploring, half condescending.

"Seventeen."

He turns and begins to soften the next stream of color with the flame.

A wave of tenderness and astonishment laps over me.

Luis turns so his face is hidden from me, and he carefully torches an area I've glazed rose.

"So you weren't even thirteen when you went up on the mountain," I say. "And your sister?"

"Fifteen."

I need something to do with my hands. I begin to mix some more color. Rich, dark color, dark as I can make it. I mix together all the deep shades and add the oil drop by drop.

"Well. I'm sure you know him better than I do," I say, when I think it's safe.

Luis doesn't answer for a while.

"That's one of the reasons he wanders so much," he says finally. "You know, patrolling used to order our days. No one would admit it, but you could feel the air go kind of electric when a patrol came back with some news. Any news. Sometimes Javier and his lieutenants would read their tracks and their garbage like entrails and move camp. But mostly they'd just laugh and dig in deeper. The police made Javier laugh more than once. They made him whistle, in appreciation, the way he'd whistle at a nasty storm or an unbroken horse. They earned his respect. Without them, we were just fools."

The window next to the window Luis is working on is pocked with sunbursts of radiating cracks, as though it has been stoned or shot at. I begin to circle one of the flaws with my brush. Soon it's a face.

"You are a little like her," Luis ventures. "Although she was certainly younger . . ."

"And more traditional, I'd imagine."

"Yes, and more traditional. But very loyal. Knew right from wrong."

At this, my brush falters, but he doesn't see.

"You see, our maternal grandmother was very British, very proper and practical. I think this helped protect Maite from that morbidity trip that drew so many to the mountains. It wasn't that different from your sixties, some say, except we never had your optimism, your innocence. Picking up a gun was not a strange thing for a well-educated teenager in my country to do. In a way, it was something we'd suspected we would have to do all along, something they just hid from us for a while—like sex, and taxes. Where I come from, we feel promise is always giving way to disaster. And the way some people are made, well, sometimes there is nothing left for a person but to be proud of this." He pauses. "They tell me it really is easier than you think to kill."

I can't tell much about the face I'm painting except that it has young eyes and a heavy jaw. Behind its temples I make out the midreaches of the low mountain range to the north. This face is still without gender.

There are going to be other faces.

"My sister was really more moderate and level-headed than most of them," Luis continues. "She came to the group slowly, consciously, and deliberately; to an extent because he had convinced her of the justness of his cause, but mainly because she'd come to the conclusion that her place was beside him.

"At home we all used to see her sitting up nights. She'd spread her hands out on her desk, flat like this, you know, and just look out the window. Into the darkness. Sometimes she would write letters, but she sat, mostly. If I interrupted her I would see I had roused her from a very complicated train of thought. When she read, she read history. This from a girl who had planned to study agricultural economy at the university and raise five children. She was not even mature for her age, not really, although she looked it. But in those few months she gained many years. You could see it. Actually see it."

He sits back on his heels and scratches his forehead.

When he speaks again, he's looking at the floor. "One day she simply didn't come home. We found a note telling us she was safe and not to worry. My parents were shocked, even though so many of their friends had been through the same thing. But Maite; so dutiful, so responsible. She took hardly anything, just some clothes."

My face is done. It's the face of a young man with curly hair; a wide-eyed, surprised face I don't know.

I start to outline another flaw in the glass. Adam slips off my brush and onto the window.

The wind is beginning to kick up tufts of foliage in the tobacco-colored fields below. The sky is clouding up flint gray and soon the first drops of rain hit the glass. The blue-gold flame and the hiss of the butane soothe me like an indoor fire on a cold winter's day. A few quick strokes and Adam is done.

Luis switches the butane off.

"Who is that?" he asks pointing at the figure.

"An old friend."

"And that?"

"I don't know."

I paint swiftly and outside the rain falls even more swiftly.

"Are you annoyed?" Luis asks.

"Not with you. Of course not. With Javier."

"Take it easy."

"Did they come for you?" I say evenly.

He looks down and scratches his head. "No. Never. Javier didn't want my sister around; me less. She followed him, and I followed her. Only I knew where she had gone. I was afraid that someone would come and beat it out of me. And it tore me up to see the folks look at me with those bewildered deer eyes. As if I had taken her myself. Just because I knew. They wouldn't say anything, they just treated me like I was a beloved monster. I freaked, I just freaked. I was afraid I would make a mistake. Of course, once I was up there I would endanger myself and everyone else if I left again, so they had to keep me around. But I hadn't thought that far."

"Me neither," I murmur.

We exchange glances. The intimacy is uncomfortable. We both start working again. Los Anenomes in the rain is comforting. The green light washes through our colored windows and softens the white walls. It's cavelike, and the air is full of movement and wetness.

Luis picks up the other brush, very tentatively. He says, "I studied drawing for a while."

"Was she glad to see you?"

"Angry. Some kids brought me in. Luckily, one recognized me from school. She was sleeping and I reached out and woke her and she was furious at first, like I'd been spying on her. But I was angrier." He spoke these last words defiantly, as if he were afraid I would contradict him.

"I bet Javier was angry when he saw her."

"No. That was strange. They told me that when Javier saw her he cried. Maite and her backpack of sweaters and blankets. We still have one of the blankets. We haven't needed to use it yet. It hasn't been that cold."

Luis speaks agreeably, as if Maite is traveling in India and will be back to pick up the blanket soon.

Luis is painting two faces on his window. One belongs to a woman, the other to a man. Both have dark, frightened eyes yet are also vaguely comical.

Back in her worst days, Elise used to fill up whole pads with little penciled faces. Endless profiles, full

faces, three-quarters; a hand to the mouth, hair caught
in a knot, loose, dark, blond, it didn't matter, it was all
the same elegant little face with perfect rosebud lips,
sloping nose, and rounded eyes. Eventually she'd crum-
ple up each page and throw it away. Whatever information the faces might have contained, she did not
consider it to be information of the permanent sort. She
would have felt at home with Los Anenomes' original
residents. She didn't leave a mark, either.

We're the kind who do. That we have in common,
the three of us up here.

"What were the others like?" I say.

"Good kids. Strong hearts. One, Tiberio, I saw
crossing the street in Madrid about a month ago. Funny
how people who go together show up over the world.
He pretended not to recognize me and I understood
that."

I understand, too. I remember the Luis who'd just
been killing time in Javier's new apartment, a Luis
whose expression always registered somewhere between pleading and bored as he managed to convey
how uncomfortable it felt to be wearing shoddy clothes
and to be thrown in with small-time hustlers. It's tough
to be held accountable for a life you know is just a life
in passing.

"Later I found out they call Tiberio the Grandfather
now, although no one could explain why. I used to go
to school with his cousin. I had a thing for her. Scrappy
little brunette, always singing. But she's gone now.
There was an incident."

Now Luis's window is filling up with more comical
little faces, faces with fat dots for eyes and half smiles.
While I've painted my faces in a way that makes them
seem to be looking out the window, his seem to be

looking in. One or two of Luis's faces, also smiling, are blindfolded. A third, the face of a boy wearing a shiny earring, is scarred. The scar and the blindfolds are cracks in the glass that Luis is repairing with his brush as he makes them part of his portraits. Smaller than the rest, in one corner, is a stick figure of a girl waving a machine gun above her head. She looks far away and precarious as though the machine gun were really a kite string, and she was flying the kite on a hilltop, with her face to the wind.

"Weren't you afraid?" I say.

Luis smiles. "Just of saying something wrong."

I stop painting.

"Well. There wasn't time. Maybe in my sleep."

The rain portions out its soft wet spurts on the outside of the glass. The faces flicker and glow.

Luis puts his brush down and lights the flame. Then, in one long, fluid movement he passes it over the window and the faces shine and liquefy and become one with the glass.

"It is a terrible thing to lose a sister," Luis says.

"A sister or a brother," I agree.

Luis nods. "Many lost brothers, too."

He closes the shutters and leaves the house by the front door, walking in the direction of the car.

CHAPTER TWELVE

⸺⸺⸺ ◇ ⸺⸺⸺

In the morning the music comes back.

I'm outside the house when it starts. It's soft, and seems to be coming from somewhere close by. Neither of the men is in sight.

Two guitars are lilting and two men are singing. The melody is almost joyful, yet the words that carry the joy are these: *Corazón, pasión, martírio, quebranto.* Heart, passion, martyrdom, sorrow.

All morning as I work the guitar song continues. I can feel it sinking deep into my nerves.

At lunch both men are unusually gloomy and silent. No one mentions the music, and I don't ask. But that afternoon the guitars are back again.

Later, Luis and I meet on the hill.

"You know," he says suddenly, "I found this book about gardens in this house where we stayed, and they talked about those flower bouquets people used to send each other where each flower sent a different message." He stops and toes a hole in the grass. "You know what anemones meant if you found some in your bouquet? They meant withered hopes."

◊

"Luis didn't have his wits about him when he showed up here," Javier says.

It's after dinner and we're playing cribbage on a magnetized travel board. I like having to look very carefully to follow the movement and configuration of the pegs in the starlight. I like the small scale and the precision required by the task.

"I never saw a kid smoke so many cigarettes. Philosophizing to himself." He counts four pegs by touch and moves forward. "Letting himself be confused by small things. Taking it all in."

I'm dealing. Javier looks at me over the cards.

"Not that there wasn't a lot to take in. I'm never quite sure about Luis. Sometimes I think he is the perfect employee. Others, no."

He watches carefully for a reaction, but I can't tell if he thinks he's gotten one, or not.

"But he and I, we need each other. The problem with Luis is that he's still too much of a kid to know what he loves in life. He could have loved it here as well as anywhere." He gestures at me with his head. "The way you have those glass candlesticks."

"Hurricane lamps," I correct. But I let the rest of what he's said go by. The white faces of our cards match each other on the grass. It's nice to have this silent moment, as equals.

I let my eyes rest on his hands as Javier counts out his crib. They give me a pleasure I can't explain, the faint echo of that innocent yet shadowy infatuation for some older and wiser man I never experienced as an adolescent—except Javier is not that much older than I.

Now he lays down the seven of hearts and glances at me carefully, gauging my reaction.

"Where did you learn to make those candlesticks?"

"Oh . . ." I pause.

"Is that how you hope to earn a living?"

The light condescension in that word, *hope,* puts me on guard. The circumstances under which we've come to know each other mean there are large gaps in the essential information each of us possesses about the other. Subtle cruelty is inflicted, from time to time, from such ignorance. It's easy to inflict, like stepping on a hand in the dark. For Javier, a young woman floating along, receptive to change, is a young woman in danger. But it isn't that way for me. I suppose every life has its own Ice Age that enhances its direction in a stunning and unimaginable way. Certainly Javier's and Luis's did. And I think mine's thawing now, in a river of icy glass in a southern country on the edge of a sea.

"You should think about it," Javier says gently. "Making a living from that. You have a feeling."

We play two rounds in silence.

"It's complicated, the glass thing," he says. "You like that, don't you?"

"You have to get to know it, I guess," I say. "Then it's like anything else. It's like practicing the piano. Do it enough times and you get the piece right."

"No, it isn't just like anything else. Fifteen-two, fifteen-four, fifteen-six. I deal."

The logic of the cards and the game give conversation a soothing atmosphere. It's like being seated near a group of nice strangers in a restaurant.

"Luis is helping you with your windows, isn't he?"

"Yes," I say. "Is there something wrong with that?"

"No. Why would you think that?"

"The way you said it."

He pauses, and I watch him weigh his reply while our suits and numbers match each other in the grass.

"At one time I would have considered your window painting dangerous to us until we find out what happened to that shipment. But not anymore." He shrugs, nodding back toward the trailer, which gleams dull silver in the trace of carbony shine that clings to the air in the new moon. " 'It was in the hills that I first found peace, first found cover, first knew death, and first understood that there were others, in the distance, taking their marks, finding me. Now I am at peace again.' An old cowboy I knew used to say that. It took me a long time to understand what he meant. But there is a lot of wisdom in those words. A lot of wisdom." He breaks off, with an almost childlike glint of satisfaction in his eyes.

"And what *is* your concept of danger?"

"That's for a different evening. Let's just say I know they're out there." He grins, a sardonic grin of satisfaction. "I know them and they know me."

Javier shuffles the deck slowly and with great effort, frowning as he pushes bent corners straight.

"Luis has made a mess out of his life. I should cut him loose until he smacks into something and pulls himself together."

"That's awfully harsh, isn't it?" I ask. "From what I understand, Luis was in a very difficult position . . ." I trail off, at a loss.

Unexpectedly, Javier grins. "Is that what he told you?" he says.

I'm silent.

"It is," he says almost triumphantly. "Son of a bitch. That son of a bitch. What exactly *did* he say?" Javier looks amused. "Never mind." He examines my face closely. "Did he tell you how his sister died?"

I shake my head.

"I didn't think so."

We play a round.

"Listen to me. Let me explain to you how to handle a certain kind of man. If a certain kind of man attempts to take liberties with you, of any kind, go straight for the jugular. There is no reason why life should not be completely correct. Why anyone should force you to do anything."

"So you're going to let me decide, are you?"

"Decide what?"

"Fifteen, eight, fifteen-twelve, home," I say, and to my surprise the game is mine.

CHAPTER THIRTEEN

◇

In the morning as I pass the furnished room in Los Anenomes I notice the locked wardrobe is standing ajar. A patterned blanket lies folded inside. Stepping closer, I see a case of audio tapes wrapped in the blanket. Each box is labeled with words that seem like they might go with the songs I've heard. The hand is clear and neat and precisely punctuated. It takes me a minute to recognize the unusually wide and symmetrical fountain-penned letters as those I saw on the photograph I came across in the glove compartment of Javier's car.

The silence intensifies, the way it does when someone is watching you. I turn and leave.

◇

That night I'm awakened by the sound of cloth rustling and quiet taps, the patient, animal-like sounds humans make in the darkness. A flashlight throws a circle of light against the eastern wall.

Barely conscious, I wonder who is up. It's the third time I've heard one of the men rising and dressing in the night, and each time I've entertained the unlikely possibility that it's Javier making his way to me. When I'm sleepy and only half aware, the lush calm of the mild night gives me a deep sense of safety that blossoms into desire.

I hear a click, a snap, a throat clearing so quietly it holds no tonality. Then a match is struck and the air fills with tobacco smoke.

I decide it's Luis who's up, because only he smokes in the trailer. He lets himself out the door and walks quickly east, toward the boat.

I get up to use the bathroom. On the way back I see the smudge of the lit cigarette bobbing silently over Luis's bed.

"Tess," he whispers.

I was wrong, it's Javier who's gone.

"Who else would it be?" I answer automatically.

"Can't you sleep?" The note of concern in Luis's voice would ordinarily be charming, but in these circumstances it makes me feel caught. Clucking and fussing comes easily to Luis. He's the most expressive of us three. Since he's usually so aloof, when this part of him comes up I'm still surprised.

"Yes. I can sleep."

I watch the tip of his cigarette glow brighter.

"I can't," he says. "I've been beating up my pillow for hours."

"Oh?" I realize he's still standing and make my way back to my bed. I sit down on the edge.

The cigarette brightens again. I make out the yellow hair, the two skinny knees holding up the plaid blanket like a tent. Luis, longing for sympathy the way a plant longs for water.

I wish I were still between the Formica sides of my bunk, which have come to seem as thick and shielding as the walls of a medieval town. But now that I'm up I have to know where Javier has gone.

"What do you miss?" Luis asks.

"Miss? About what?"

"About your land," he says softly and clearly, as if talking to a child. He uses the Spanish word *tierra,* which means earth, property, domain, and only lastly, country, when Luis and Javier use it.

It takes me a while to answer. Even in the middle of the night on an isolated hill I want to take it seriously.

"The buffers," I say finally. "Good heating in the winter, air conditioning in the summer. Fire exits. The feeling someone has thought about your safety, and provided for it, so you don't have to worry about it yourself. And privacy. In my country we're used to a lot of privacy. And loneliness, too, that's the flip side."

Two long drags on the cigarette, a pumping up and down of the knees. "Oh. I see. Dulling the impact. In the United States they dull the impact." He gets out of his bed and paces the passageway in his cut-offs. He throws his arms out and up like a performer acknowledging an audience. "This," he says, "is the impact." He turns around and waves the cigarette at me. "Right?"

"I suppose." I'm groggy, and not ready for a performance. I'm still wondering where Javier has gone.

"Won't you join me?" Luis is pouring Johnnie Walker into two tin cups. I decide either Javier's absence does not interest him or he is deflecting my interest with charm.

But handing me the cup, he says, "Our friend went out looking for an impact fix, just now." Again, the crisp pronunciation I have never noticed in the daytime.

"Looking?" Now I am fully awake. "You mean on patrol?"

Luis sits down alongside me and hands me my tin cup of Scotch. "That boyfriend of yours. He invents problems where they don't exist. He puts himself in danger and thinks he's making himself safe."

"Can you be a little more specific?" The iciness in my own voice catches me off guard.

"Certainly." He pats my knee and sips halfheartedly at the Scotch. "Every night, as you may have noticed, one or the other of us goes on a midnight stroll. A little patrol. Your boyfriend is waging a little battle within. Half of him says, "I must take care because some half-crazed policeman from halfway across the world may hunt me down. I don't want to, but I have no choice.' That is the Javier we love. The other half of him says, 'THEY are here, waiting. They will kill everything and everyone I love, so I will love no one. And if I cannot hunt them down, well, then I will let them know I know them. If I am sacrificed, it is no loss. We will all be sacrificed. If not in cold blood, then like those wild little desert children in their birthday suits.' Has he told you about them yet? Well, then you have something to look forward to.

"This is the Javier who comes to Los Anenomes for a little R and R. A little R and R hideout. This is the Javier who makes us patrol his Magic Mountain. Can't patrol the condo, someone'd tut-tut. This is the man who half hopes they'll shoot him dead. And who likes to say, 'You don't know you're really alive until you kill someone.' Or until you experience the sensation of walking through the night looking for death yourself."

Luis shakes his head. "I myself have never seen anything but a stray cow and some lizards. Once I even took a nap under one of those trees near the stream, but he came up behind me and scared me to death. He even patrols his own patrols. It's easier just to do it than to argue with him." With his hand, he draws circles in the air around his head. "But it's completely crazy. How could one man walking all the hills for two pitiful hours of the night protect himself from some son-of-a-bitch nasty evil that he thinks stalked him halfway across the world?" He breaks off.

"Luis, there is one thing I don't understand." My voice sounds newly fluid, silvery, cool. "If he's crazy, and we're bait, then why are you still here?"

He puts his finger on my lips and looks at me sadly. "Someday I'll tell you."

"Tell me now."

He rests the flat of his hand on my knee. "Things have changed since that day we talked. I don't want to leave anymore. That . . . that was self-indulgence. I just wanted to get to know you."

I've been doing the best I could to prevent either of them from drawing me into the darker hyperbole of this rivalry they seem to have: that dark place we all have that requires attention to grow the way fire needs oxygen. I decide to say as little as possible now.

"Just tell me this," I whisper. "Are we here for a good reason? Does this really have to do with the shipment and your friend Danny? Just tell me that."

He looks at me, and his eyes are half shut and shining.

"Oh no," he says. "Danny really got arrested. This game is not about what happens, it's about how Javier interprets. It's him. It's him. So let me give you a piece of advice. Tread gently."

"Luis, what's this Danny like?"

"Well, let's see. Nice guy, smart. Blond. Wears a diamond earring. I don't know, a regular guy."

He tucks his hand around my shoulder. It's cool and soothing and that's all it takes for me to feel like heaven. I lay my head on his shoulder. The posture is easy and familiar; Luis himself feels utterly comfortable and calm. Something about his words is striking a chord, too.

"Everyone needs the illusion of order," Luis says. "To feel protected. But when your country is shot to hell or for some reason you keep skipping from one to the next . . ." He shrugs and looks at me. "Then guys like Javier come in handy. They give you a big picture where you can go about your business. Obey, disobey, love it, hate it. At least it's something to bounce off of."

Luis is running his hand up and down my arm while he tells me jokes out of a magazine he'd brought in from town. He feels cool and relaxed and compact.

"Don't worry," he whispers when I stir. "We'll be awake long before he comes home."

"Luis, who's the group singing on the tapes?"

But he doesn't answer. He seems to have drifted into sleep as easily as a child, as someone who has never experienced guilt. He feels familiar. He feels just like Adam.

CHAPTER FOURTEEN

◇

I wake up looking at Luis's cool, still face. It's as calm as the moon and translucent as a pale curtain.

I pull away from him and stretch out on the side of the bunk. Being next to him is almost like being next to no one at all—except that it's more reassuring. It's still black outside. I welcome the lightness, even mixed with danger, of being there with him, now. I run my fingers from my toes up along my body, over the slopes of my face, and reach them as far above me as they'll go. Being next to Luis is just like being in my own space. It feels the same.

And Luis understands almost everything, the way I do. But unlike me, he doesn't seem to let himself care too much about what he understands.

Confusing comprehension with compassion is a mistake I don't want to make again. Suddenly I feel less comfortable about lying on the edge of Luis's bed.

I go back to my own bunk and sit on the scratchy blue blanket. I look at my hands, take a deep breath, and try to count up the days for the first time. I come up with three weeks.

No one will be looking for me. My Spanish friends don't know me well enough to know how I usually behave. Elise on her barge is at least as inaccessible and unpredictable as I am, and Bob understands and expects my long silences. "You're like me that way," he used to say. "You need time to reconstruct yourself." Meant to be comforting, those words were more like a cold field that had to be worked alone.

I lie down and look at the sky, which is moderating into a pink-and-beige dawn. The house is almost colorless, and the grass and brush seem to absorb its hues. Without the light, my Los Anenomes windows will be sapless, distant, reproving, calm. I wonder how they'd look with only the bare bones left. What the residue will be.

I guess I'm saying, I wonder what kind of skull they have, and what I'm going to do about it.

I have to find out. That's what I'm doing here. I'm living in my glass. I'm looking for the part of me that knows myself the way Javier seems to and that also knows what to do about it.

Whatever the glass shows me, I want to admire every panel, to absorb it from every angle, unrepentant. Divested of light, what's left will be a mirror I look into after a long absence. No extra light, no extra darkness. I'll see what to do next.

I see the black-and-silver platter that made me put glass away for years, and I love it *and* my loss. All the silly little paperweights and cups Elise had strewn through her house and boats. I step out the door and head across the field.

Just then, Javier walks out of the brush at the left side of the house and slowly settles onto one of the broken steps.

I guess the watch is over. He looks very tired. If he sees me, it doesn't show.

I go still. I wonder, which Javier is this: the tempered survivor, the man who has done something, who can support all the weight of his life on his shoulders? Or, is this the man who shatters if you hit the wrong corner at the right angle? The one who can cut you, who can put you at risk. He's reminding me too much of the men I'm remembering, and I don't like it. But maybe this is what happens when desire starts to well up in that parched field; perhaps the memory colors it. Maybe I'm the one who sees things wrong.

I try to see a way around him to get inside, but I can't find one. I don't want to see him anymore: his house, his dream, his little glass horse. I want to see me. Slowly, the idea of going to the windows becomes sadly narcissistic to me. It's lost its magic. As my thoughts turn, the sun strains past the horizon and confirms them.

Javier gestures to me.

I begin to walk across the field toward him. I must be wrong about all this. I have to be. He just watches me, steady as the house itself. His eyes move over every inch of me. I wonder how I could ever have thought I recognized myself in him. He stays still. I move forward.

Then I realize, Maite followed him up a hill, too. If I can trust Luis, he went on watch for her, too.

I have to be wrong about all of this. I have to be. But perhaps desire is awakening the memories in Javier, too.

I turn around and begin to walk back to the trailer. Each step is like hauling myself through ice water but I do it anyway. I can see Javier's reflection in the trailer window, just watching and smoking. His gaze pulls at my back and then it tries to burn through me. He knows me too well. He knows what I'm thinking now, he might even know what I'm remembering but have not told him.

I close the trailer door behind me and drink in Luis's cool, still face framed against the pillow. I look outside. Javier is walking toward the car.

Silently, expertly, I unbutton my blouse and lie back beside Luis.

"Get up," I say. "Please, wake up."

Instantly, those brown eyes, alert and coy, are flickering softly over me. A soft hand reaches out to my breast, just so, as if it had cupped it a thousand times.

Luis's hands and mouth are agile and soothing, and his responses are the quick, satisfying responses of the disinterested. Later, he looks me up and down.

"There isn't a mark on either of us," he says with clear satisfaction.

CHAPTER FIFTEEN

◇

That day stays white and chill and for the first time in this waning summer it's cold enough to build a fire.

The coals glow orange in the pit. For a while all three of us stay close to them, drinking coffee and watching the fog cover the valley until even the house is nothing but a few dark windows in the atmosphere.

"No painting for me today, I guess." I kick the ground.

"Can't risk taking the boat tarp off." Luis squints at the sky. "Mmmnh mmn. Warp. Hey," he says, slapping me lightly on the forearm. "Why don't you go up to the top floor to look for more little pieces?"

"I'm heading back up the property," Javier announces, turning in the other direction.

No one speaks or moves.

"Why don't you go ahead, Luis," I say finally. "I'll be there in a minute."

Luis smiles softly and disappears into the mist.

I pour myself another cup of coffee. Javier gives me a sharp look and pours one of his own. He calls out into the mist, *"Macho,* go check to make sure the boat is dry."

I can barely see Luis, but I hear him glide by us toward the boat.

"I meant what we talked about," Javier says in a low voice when he is gone. "About us. In the gazebo."

"I knew what you meant."

Every once in a while the fog subsides and pieces of the landscape reappear. Now the first row of trees at the western edge of the field break through.

"I just wanted to know if you understood it is present in my mind."

"Yes, but things aren't so black and white for me. Maybe because my life has been a little more reliable than yours. I can enjoy the gray parts, you know?" And I add to myself, and you who are so certain of your world and your sway and so uncertain of your worthiness, you might detour me into a life that isn't my own.

"Well." Javier is irritated. "I didn't say I needed you to explain anything to me."

Luis's shadow glides back in front of us and toward the house.

"Wait up!" I call.

My footsteps sound juicy on the wet grass. At each end of them a man stands, listening. I wonder if there might not be a third way. My steps begin to sound like a horse galloping. It isn't until a moment later that I realize I really did hear the unmistakable sound of hoofs hitting turf. The horse is bearing down behind me. There is something odd about the sound, more syncopated than usual. The rhythm's off.

Behind me Javier swears.

I turn to see a dark-maned roan plunge out of the fog, head forward and tense, neck curved tight as a bow, chest round and heaving. The evergreens make a ghostly frame as she runs straightlong toward the hill and starts turning circles. She's barebacked, but loose reins hang from her bridle and slap against her side.

I back away.

Javier and Luis walk slowly forward.

"She's favoring her left fore, *jefe,*" Luis calls.

"I can see. She's out of her mind, the poor girl. She must have gotten caught up in the reins."

They approach the horse from opposite directions. Luis stops about ten feet in front of me and Javier bears in on her with strong, deliberate steps. The mare circles slowly to a soft trot. There's a rough catch to her breath and her teeth snap white in the gray air.

"Tranquila, tranquila," admonishes Javier, and then he's bracing himself against the earth and holding her neck in one hand and slipping his belt around it with the other. He grabs the reins, ties them around, and takes hold of her bridle.

"Now, *flaco,*" he calls. "She'll be easy now. Easy, my girl, easy."

Luis comes up to him. He and Javier murmur to each other and Luis stands to the far side and they walk the horse over to the closest tree. She's heaving and shivering now, and there's froth on her face and neck. Twice she stumbles and pitches forward, and twice they catch her before she falls. The last time she stumbles, I hear a soft crack. I'm surprised by the relief I feel when I see Javier and Luis are walking her over branches and twigs.

When they get to the tree Javier holds the horse and talks to her while Luis goes for rope to make a lead. They take the bridle out and replace it with their halter

186 RIVER OF GLASS

and then they tie the mare there and rub her down and
talk to her and hold her.

Finally, Javier remembers me.

"Ven," he calls. "Come on over here. Nothing to be
afraid of. Remember her? She's the sweetheart you rode
when you went out with me that morning."

I look. She doesn't seem like the same horse. That
horse was dull and plodding, while this one has arrived
like a messenger from heaven. Then I recall how sleepy
and sweet that beast was, how it followed each of Javier's moves with the greatest obedience, even when I
disagreed. This reassures me. I walk forward.

"She must have gotten loose somehow from Patricio
nearby and in the fog came here instead of home. She
follows you everywhere anyway." Luis is squinting at
her leg and Javier is holding it.

"Probably," Javier agrees. He looked almost de-
lighted while he was stalking her, but now that she's
tied his face looks hard.

I hear another of those keening cracks on the horse's
last stumble and Javier has begun to manipulate the leg
she's favoring. The horse is backing away and trying
to rear, but Luis is holding her firm. "Don't know what
the doctor would say," Javier says, but his face shows
he has made a decision. He and Luis loosen up on her
at the same time and break her fall as she tumbles to
the ground. Luis looks up.

"Don't know what to do, do you?" Luis asks.

"How in hell did she get all the way up here?" Javier
mutters.

"You rode her here sometimes, didn't you?" My
voice is clear and pleases me.

Javier looks over at me, startled that I'm the one
who's responded. He seems to have expected Luis, who
just keeps on looking at her.

"Yes," Javier says. "I did."

"So it's just like Luis said."

Javier backs away from her. He doesn't seem sure about what to do next. "You don't suppose someone sent her after me?"

Luis stands up and gives him a hard dark look. "No," he says, shortly. "Don't complicate things. Patricio let her out on a long ride with someone and she got loose."

I add, "The time I rode her she followed your every move."

The fog is thinning a little. We can see the trailer, and the house, and the first few rows of trees. Above us a bird flies by low.

The mare is all taut orbs clenching together. She stretches her head out on the ground and we watch her neck skim up and down with shallow breathing.

"I'm not sure it's broken, *jefe,*" Luis is saying when suddenly she heaves herself upright again.

"Now," Javier says in a low commanding voice. "You, Luis, behind. You, Tess, up front with me."

We obey. Luis goes white in the face. He wraps one arm around the mare's stomach and places the other on top of her flanks. He talks to her, soothing. "Come on, Tessa. Stand right across from me and put one arm on her neck and one behind her good foot. Just calm her."

The mare is arching up now, almost prancing.

"Haaaa," says Javier, and dark hot blood jets over my arms and face and into the ground. Across her neck, Javier's chest is soaked red. I cry out to him, but it's the mare who slithers down, head forward, the proud neck softening and crumpling. Her hindquarters buckle and kick at the air and then all of her falls heavily to the dirt.

"You son of a whore, you could've told us first. She kicked into me." It is Luis who finally speaks.

The ground turns red, and so does the base of the tree. The roots seem to suck up blood.

My insides shake. Utterly composed, Javier kneels next to the mare, watching the blood loosen out of her, like a man looking for the right break in traffic so he can get on a busy highway. The break comes. Softly, he leans forward and twists the knife in further.

The horse makes a small agonized sound and then her eyes go dull. Bubbles of blood mound from her mouth and nostrils.

Something steel inside centers me again and I walk away from this crime and toward Luis.

"That leg was definitely broken." Javier stands up.

"Are you all right?" I kneel down and shelter Luis from Javier.

"You'll have to throw those clothes away, Tessa. I'm sorry." I hear Javier speaking very gently. But I'm the one who feels ashamed. He stops behind me and places his hand on my neck. I freeze, but then he's inside the trailer.

"Son of a bitch, son of a bitch, son-of-a-whore murderer." Luis is still holding his middle.

"Are you okay?" I repeat.

He looks at me and blinks. Then he takes his hands away from his gut and rests them on his knees.

"Yeah," he says. "Just give me a minute. *Tú, tranquila.*"

"Why *tranquila*?" I wail. "What just happened here?"

"Just forget about it."

"I thought people *shot* horses to put them out of their misery."

"Probably thought it would attract attention."

"All the way up *here*?"

"I told you. Javier has his own private list of what's

risky and what isn't. I stopped trying to guess what was on it a long time ago. Please."

Luis sees me look at the carcass and at the dark, fertile-looking stain oozing around it.

"Please. We'll bury her. Don't worry. This happened once before. I just didn't think he'd do it again." Luis stands up slowly.

"There's another horse buried here?"

Luis nods quickly, too quickly.

"What else is buried here?"

"Nothing."

"Look, go wash up. He'll leave you alone if you want him to. He's nuts about you. Don't forget that. I'll meet you down at the house."

"Please come with me," I say. "Please." I notice the smudge on his shirt and wince at the thought of the bruise that must be forming underneath.

Luis shakes his head. "She didn't kick me hard," he says. "Go on now. Just forget about it." The end of his voice turns up into a sob and he walks away.

In the trailer an open bottle of whiskey is standing on the table and the shower is running. I've picked up my coffee cup for comfort and now I add a shot of whiskey and shake the mug around. As I lift the cup to my mouth I notice the red on my hands is caking and drying. More than most people, I don't like the sight of my own blood. I unbutton my overshirt, open the door, and throw the shirt out on the grass. I'm furious. I pour myself another drink and knock it back. The sharp taste cleanses away an increment of horror. I pour a third drink.

"Tessa."

I whirl and throw the cup at him. Then I come at him and start beating him with my fists. I can barely

see. It takes him a minute because I'm fast and deter-
mined, but he gets hold of me and backs me up against
his chest and forces me inside. "No, dammit, dammit,"
I keep repeating.

"*Venga,* yell, yell, louder," he says. "Go. Get it all
out. Tell me what an evil shit I am." He keeps an iron
grip on my wrist with one hand and with the other he
rips my bloodied T-shirt down the back and off of me.

"No," I shout as he pushes me into a room.

"Yes," he shouts back, and sits me down in the hot
running shower. Clean water rushes past my head.

My legs stretch out onto the floor. Javier crouches
down, unlaces my shoes, and pulls them off.

"Not squeamish, are you?" he asks.

"Not a bit," I murmur, the water coursing down me
and cleaning it all away.

"I didn't think so."

His eyes rest on my bare skin. I give him a cold stare
and he stops.

"How do you feel now?" he says after a pause.

"*Tolerable.*" I relish the offhand drawl that lends itself
the Spanish pronunciation of the word.

"You can think whatever you like," he says, looking
levelly into my eyes. "But it was the best thing for me
to do. You handled your part well."

"I didn't know what I was going to be doing."

"Think about it. Your problem is you never let yourself get clean again. You keep punishing yourself for
nothing. Without even knowing exactly why."

I open my eyes and look back at him.

Javier shrugs. "I'm a pretty good study of people.
Especially certain people. When you come out, I'll bring
you another cup of coffee."

When I open my eyes again I'm alone.

The shower water is getting chill. As I dry myself I remember imprinting my body with Javier's in the dark room at Los Anenomes on that night three weeks ago. The last of the few times we were together. *Quédate conmigo y vive.* Stay with me and stay alive.

I dress. The fresh coffee is waiting for me on the table, as Javier promised, and the whiskey bottle is gone. I stop to drink the coffee, starting the morning over again. Then, carefully averting my eyes from the carcass under the tree, I run through the field and toward the house where Luis and the piece of glass are waiting.

Inside the door, as I move through the dark ballroom, I hear Luis rustling upstairs. Small, intermittent scrapes.

The house feels different. Quiet. I remember the first thing I'd wanted to do that morning and switch course. I float my way through the house to the smallest of the front three parlors and begin lavishing the glass with deep-red flowers from a can of color left over from the day before. The blossoms come quickly: some as small and closed as my fist; others long-petaled, indolent, almost translucent. They all pulse with light; I'm lost in an indecent rain of sprays and buds. Color rushes out of me. And I stand back now and then, as amazed as if the windows were singing. I am doing something.

Perhaps the fourth or fifth time I do this I see half a face moving out from behind one of my brightest creations.

It's a real face, not a painted face. And it's not a face I know.

Don't react, I tell myself, do. I put down my brush and begin to walk through the back of the house more quickly than I ever thought possible.

CHAPTER SIXTEEN

⸻ ◇ ⸻

The fear buoys me along. So Luis was wrong, there is someone here and Javier is my protector. He is out in front of the house, sitting against the trunk of an orange tree.

"Someone is here. Someone looked in at me through the windows in the front of the house. Not Luis."

He glances up at me sideways to shield his eyes from the sun.

"Who?"

I kneel on the grass. "I'm not sure," I whisper. The milky sun seeps through the thinning clouds onto my neck and hands. "Somebody dark with short hair. On the other side of the window I was painting."

"A man?"

"I think so." I try to recall the features. They seemed masculine, but I had only a glimpse through the red flowers.

"Did he see you?"

"I'm not sure."

"There was no light inside?"

This isn't the reaction I expected. "No." I look out at the hills and the thick waving green brush. "I guess he could be anywhere," I say. I think, how can daylight be so full of eyes?

"Kids used to come here."

"Should I get Luis?"

Javier shrugs. He stands up and walks away from his tree, right out into the open meadow, and puts his hands on his hips. My eyes follow him, but my feet are still. I feel eyes everywhere, I see danger pulsing across the meadow like white heat-lightning.

Javier turns and looks at me, waiting for me to join him. But I feel better behind the tree. I am confused and I am frightened. He looks back with disapproval, then turns away, walking.

I lift my face. Air around trees is always cooler and thicker. For a moment I imagine climbing up into the branches to wait for Javier to come back. But the ground offers more avenues of escape. I imagine hanging this tree with bits of glass and ornament. This distracts me from my fear.

"It was a kid." Javier is behind me.

"How do you know?" I don't turn around.

He comes and faces me, rocking forward on the balls of his feet, amused by my rigid posture, gauging me. If he wanted me to stay right where I was, there wouldn't be anything I could do about it. I know that's what he's thinking. Some people are just like that, always assessing their odds. For them, it's like seeing or hearing.

"Little tiny footprints." His voice is almost teasing. "Just a little guy looking for a place to piss."

"Is he gone?"

"There are some broken branches. An ice cream wrapper."

"Will you show me?"

He raises an eyebrow.

"I rubbed them out." He gestures behind him with his head. "I'm going to take a walk. Want to come?"

If I go it will be the first time we spend real time alone together since I was with Luis. There is a tightness in my back and a wind blowing in my head. So this is how Javier always feels. Anything can be a sign. Or danger. Or rescue. Or deliverance. At least walking, my body will move along with my mind and I can slow them down together.

"It's hard to trust you." I hate being in the open, where the eyes can watch us. I must trust Javier completely; my safety is in his hands. And right now I can't. I can't get a fix on him, or on me. Or on the past or the present. There is too much all wrapped up together here, and too much of it is unsaid, or unclear. I know soon I'll be in the decisive moment, the one where if I stay with them any longer I'll never be able to go back. Back to my simple white room, to my kiln and my lamps, back to slipping easily in and out of each day and each world and toward the next. The world is thawing for me, and I must be on top of things, I must shape the current and where the river goes. But now it won't be as easy as using my hands or my breath. I must do something.

Most people don't have the luxury of weighing a choice that changes their lives: something just happens, branches snap underfoot. You fall through the trapdoor. But despite or perhaps because of the hardship that's caused this fall, in the new world where you find yourself all the complexity you have known melts into new simplicity.

I think of Maite sitting at her bedroom desk night after night and staring into space with those liquid, dark eyes. I know those eyes: their clarity, their stubbornness, the mossy current of concern and conscience. The issues are not the same ones, and neither are the risks. But Maite had the same luxury I have: the luxury of choice. No trapdoors for her, either. I think that for Maite at the end love had very little to do with it. No one's eyes were open wider than hers when she left her note, packed up her blankets and her music, walked outside, hitched a ride to the hill, and delivered herself.

There's a jet overhead. The sun, growing stronger, is heating our backs. The fog is melting away. Javier keeps walking.

"*It was in the hills that I first found peace, first found cover, first knew death, and first understood that there were others, in the distance, taking their marks, finding me. Now I am at peace again.* It confers power," Javier says, shooting another glance at me, "to think you have written such a thing yourself that many others are saying. That's what we had just said, when Luis lost his sister. It was early in the morning, like this."

"How did they find you?" It no longer matters who "they" are.

"Luis. He was on watch. He'd convinced us he was worthy and we let him. He'd been lost in one of his wonderful thoughts and he showed those *locos* the way and they came back with him. They'd been just waiting to pounce. She was standing at the edge of camp. Armed. Worried about him. Collecting wood, for dinner.

"It was quick. I heard gunfire and I came running, but I could do nothing. I was just in time to see her go down. She'd fired first, to warn us. She'd seen them before anyone."

Javier has averted his face from me. He is speaking his words carefully downwind and away from the hill, as if they were bullets or flames. "When he wants to, that Luis has the instincts of a fox. He just disappeared."

Abruptly, Javier changes direction and walks down the side of the hill, quickening his pace. I follow. Then he weaves back up again. We keep going like that, back and forth. His voice goes on, louder, and inflected with a speeding cadence. "We couldn't even give her a funeral. I watched them. I watched them drag her away. Their hands . . . on her, Luis never saw that," Javier said. "There's a lot that little fox never saw." He flashed his eyes back at me and I flinched. He registered my reaction by setting his jaw and then he looked away again and I could tell he was trying to rein in his voice. "She's the one who keeps him here, you know.

"I led away off the mountain all those I could. And then I left the lot of them. For two months I wandered out in the *pampas* half crazy, daring them to come and get me. But they never did. Finally there was nothing to do except to let it lift away. Then I knew it was time to go, that I had poured all my craziness out on the fields. But I still remember our old prayer."

I wish I'd stayed behind the tree.

I have been waiting so long to find out what the knot is that ties him and Luis together and brought them here. I thought it would explain once and for all who is right and who is wrong, who is safe and who is dangerous. But he's told me, and nothing's changed. Although, as Luis said last night, it doesn't have to matter. Everyone needs the illusion of order. While you do what you have to do, regardless. Repair windows. Mourn. Try to shape a country, far away. Everyone expects a sky of stars to plot a course by. Especially when that first sky has been erased, contorted. Then you're hungrier for order, and less particular about its source. You become a pragmatist. Sometimes, like Javier, you get so pragmatic you supply the order yourself. That's harder, though. Because then you need people underneath to plot their course by you. Then you need someone who will always come with you when you invite them on a walk.

"Are we hiding out in the open now?" I ask.

"Yes. I think so. I am, anyway. You, it seems, are hiding in Luis."

I look over at him. He's watching a crow coast down the valley. I want to be able to touch him and to back away and yet I know that beneath he isn't vulnerable at all: he's a magnet, and if I touch him I'll stick.

"When I came here I spent six months in the bleakest corner of Extremadura. Breeding horses. Seeing nobody. Thinking nothing. Bands of crazy, naked children in the desert there. Playing."

Right then, I decide. I'm not going to disappear into her, into him. I'm not going to hide my darkness in his, I'm not going to hide my light in the light of a world no one will ever see.

I hear myself saying, "Let them have you if you want, but I won't let you get me. I can be safe. I can help you be safe. Being up here doesn't mean shit. I don't know about last time, but this time you're wasting it. You're wasting Luis. You're wasting me. You're wasting."

He turns his face back toward me. His body follows his eyes and his eyes are on fire and then his hands are on my shoulders and he's mumbling. "You to say," I hear, "who are you"; the full weight of him bears down.

I try to shift my feet as they cut into the soft ground.

I step back and back. "Whoa," I say. "Stop." I can't
tell if he is pushing me or embracing me. Then we are
rolling over and over in the brush and dirt. "Whoa," I
repeat. He tries to pin me and I can't tell if he is trying
to overpower me or put out my fear. I can't see his face
anymore, just a neck and arms grasping. *"Javier,"* I call.
He's too far away. He stops my leg with his leg. I hit
his jaw hard with the back of my hand. He grabs my
arm and holds it behind me, stopping just short of
twisting it. I can feel the knife in his pocket, and the
second blade in his boot. "Just go ahead and use it if
you're going to." My own voice sounds low and harsh
to me.

Javier's eyes narrow. He raises his free hand and slaps
me twice, once on either side of my face. He pushes his
knee between my legs and pries them apart. Coughing,
I pry my fingers into his pocket and come out with the
heavy blade in my hand. He pushes harder against me
as I pry it open. I can feel my own blood running down
my fingers. He can't get hold of my knife hand. He's
trying but I can't tell how hard he's trying. Every time
he gets near, I manage to get it away. His face is just a
shadow and I want to rip it off of him, cut it off, cut it
away.

"Loca, anda, loca, matarás a todos," I hear him saying.
"You're killing us," I whisper, "you're leaving us
open." His knife in my hand finds a soft place near his
neck and sighs in.

His hands wrap tight around my neck and I can feel
their warmth and softness.

I pull the knife out of him and slide it under a green
tangle and we hold on to each other. We roll down the
lee of the hill, and I can feel the small, iron hands, distracted, and taste the blood and the dirt and he is trying
to hold me to him as he holds his life inside him.

Slowly I move my hand to his neck and touch the opening I have made. I place my hand over it. I dance my palm over the pressure, savoring it and controlling it. He puts his hand over mine and when we take our hands away the flow slows. His eyes are on me. They're changed. They're softer, more watchful. They're intently interested. They seem to think I have something they want.

"I'll get Luis," I whisper.

And as I run back up the hill, I understand that even though I tried to get free, the long descent is over and I'm one of them now.

CHAPTER SEVENTEEN

◇

"You have to come with me," I say to Luis. "Now."

He follows me away from the boat and across the field. I want always to be ahead. That way by the time he finds the body I'll already be beyond it and I'll know what happens next.

Come with me, I think. I'm leading you there.

I look at the soft brush that covers the ground and picture the life feeding on life underneath.

"Hurry," I call, and my hands began to pull deep gulps of air, rungs of wind. Luis catches up. He touches my fingers once, and pulls away.

"Down the hill," I explain. The hill is longer than I remember, much longer, and covered with a sheen of tiny blue flowers. The blue growth seems to quiver. I try to make myself stop thinking about flowers. I am Tess Jordan and with my body and my touch and my pulse I raise stakes higher than they are meant to be. I sense the hurricanes in others and draw them out before their time. The flowers' scent lifts up to me and embraces me and it is the heavy blue-and-green scent of thyme.

There is Javier, just beyond.

Luis says, "He's alive."

I pull the second knife out of his boot. It's polished so brightly I can see myself in it, but I don't look. It's not because I'm afraid I'll look different. It's because I know I'll look exactly the same.

"I thought he was going to use it on me. And it was like there was already a line from my hand to his throat. It was almost like he'd set things up so I'd hurt him. Like he wanted me to." I think about Maite, and about the first night we spent here, when he asked me to bury him in sawdust. I walk back out to where Luis is fixing a tent around Javier with one of the boat tarps. Javier is still unconscious. "I guess there's probably more to it, though." I fall silent, watching Luis minister to him. Luis knows what he's doing. This doesn't surprise me. "You know, after the mare and what happened to your sister and everything and us being together. I just didn't know." There is more to it than that, too, but I haven't mentioned this part to Luis or Javier. It's back in what I've been remembering.

"Sometimes we all wanted that to happen. He knew it, too. He knew how many people wanted to hurt him. Pay him back. For changing our lives. Not that it was his fault, personally. When he started getting tortured that way, even more."

"But I was the one who actually did it. And I wasn't even there on that mountain."

Luis looks up. "I guess you just want to live," he

observes, glancing at my body. "Nothing wrong with that."

I pull my shirt tighter around me. "I guess you're right. I guess I do." I sit down. "I guess there isn't," I add. The ground pulses under my hands, my hips. I shape my thoughts to that pulse, easing, easing.

Just then Javier's eyes open and stay open for a while. They hold a very particular look of clear attention, of unbiased, open awareness. They frighten me and they make me sad. I feel like I'm going to be sick.

"He should heal," says Luis. He comes up behind me and touches my back, just to let me know he's there. His hands feel different: proprietary, as if I belong to him or to what I have done and must be protected. And they are also trying to reacquaint themselves with me.

"Come on," I reply finally. "You know what this feels like. This is what happened to you on the mountain. You know more about this than I do. I'm just beginning to catch up." I'm afraid to say what I mean by "this" out loud, but Luis knows: getting in over your head. Being caught by the breaking glass. Doing something about it you wish you hadn't had to, which marks you forever.

He smiles. "Maybe I'm just happy that I need you to remember how it used to be."

"This is perverse. You're getting off on how it used to be."

"Being smart helps," says Luis gently, "at a time like this." He bends over Javier one more time and says, "It's clean, I think."

Javier's eyes open again and their soft attention turns to me. It's a look of clear suffering. I can feel a deep pull toward him, and a lighter higher pull away. He closes his eyes again.

I remember him saying: "You don't know you are truly alive until you have killed someone."

I am holding on to the string that centers the world with just my will. Holding on gently, but not letting go. In control. I've done something. He's reacted to me.

Letting out the darkness has different effects on different people. It can be as intimate and revealing as how they move in bed, as the relationship between a person and the art that person makes. Letting out the darkness in me has made me a child.

We were bound as deeply and secretly as mother and child. If he lived, neither of us would ever feel alone again.

Not to know your light from your darkness but to keep on going, day by day, until you do. That's the hardest test.

I know because of how things were after Lars died. My feeling for glass kept flowing then. I didn't really see what I was making. I just followed feelings. But those feelings made light and shine and depth and sharpness fall into patterns that leading held in place the way nerves limn the mind.

I recognized them as the countless shadows I had inside of me. But I also discovered how when I let them out they cast and recast themselves inside beams of light, gently and needlessly flickering, like the gentle but terrifying shadows of a high shade tree in the late afternoon that come up behind you as unexpectedly as your own darkness.

And slowly the house on the hill filled up with illuminated shadows of mine, these shadows contained so perfectly by glass I could see every terrifying nuance. Soon, in our house, I could see those shadows everywhere. Bottled shadow on the end tables, window shadow on the walls, in the kitchen a deep curved gray platter of shadow sheltering a dozen night-purple plums.

At night I woke up and saw traces of myself where the moon picked up the nerves and hollows of the pieces that lined my room. And mornings I'd be entranced by the light-borne shadows surrounding me. I was stunned by the awful narcissism of my own darkness.

It was a private punishment. The details of the work saved me. I kept myself safe protecting myself. I spun the shadows out and sealed myself in.

In a way, the glasswork had displaced Adam.

It had been too much for us after what happened to his father. Our need for each other was like an amusement park tilt-a-whirl. The big wheel starts out spinning level to the ground, and strapped into your small compartment you tell yourself it doesn't seem so bad. But slowly the ride begins to angle up perpendicularly and you are defying gravity. That was how it had been with Adam and me. The night we drove into the city to the hospital was the last night. It was also the only night we actually slept in the same bed together. The Apfels brought him back to our house. An hour or so after everyone went to bed, he groped into my bedroom as if he had been in search of a glass of water but turned the wrong way.

He stood there for a minute on the rag rug, lost and exposed even in the darkness.

I had been awake anyway, wondering and listening and feeling aroused. I felt safe and protected in the cool sheets. I remembered how until then the world had seemed to fall into order when we were touching.

I was drawing him to me without doing a thing. He was moving slowly across the rug, slowly along the floor. It seemed to take forever.

And then he was pushing himself inside me, harder and faster than he had ever done. He held my arms down with his fists. I felt the purr inside I'd felt that afternoon, and then the purr lifted and grew into a tunnel that reached farther and farther and he was following it, up and up, until it burst into a kind of running water or glass, melting, and he breathed in sharply and floated until we were both far, far away.

We shrank and came back.

He pulled away from me.

I lay on his shoulder.

Neither of us knew what to do with our hands. We moved them everywhere, but anywhere was the wrong place for them to be.

The silence of the house became impossible. I felt him everywhere in my bed. I wanted him out. It was my bed. I felt his discomfort, which compounded my own. We took our hands away from each other. This went on for what seemed like hours.

I looked over at him and saw that he was crying. Tears glistened down his face and his neck. When he saw me looking he turned his head away.

"I've got to go," he huffed, pulling on the pair of Lars's pajamas Elise had given him. And then he stumbled out the door and down the hall.

That was how Adam and I got off the tilt-a-whirl. The next time I saw him was at breakfast, with my mother. New people were there, telling her about the others on their way. No one noticed Adam and I were white and worn as parchment, which was just as well. We spent the day standing next to each other, pale and reserved and silent and feeling like we were grown-ups who had suffered each other's flaws for years. Then Mariah came with John, and I watched him turn fifteen again as he disappeared through the door.

That made the ground feel firm again. And it solved an old mystery for me. During the year I had lived with Bob, the year Adam left for Mariah's, Lars must have been behaving all the time the way he had that afternoon in New York.

By winter of that year life had quieted down. And I had gotten used to my new self. Soon I would be out of high school and away. People stopped looking at us all with such concern. I was finally used to this new element, this glass that was becoming as constant yet as mutable in my life as air and water. I got so accustomed that fish started swimming through the glass I made as if it really were water and air. As if glass were a basic element of the world, and not something people had to make at all.

Not real fish. Fish I made. Glass fish I set free, wriggling into the deep shining pleasure of the future: fuchsia and blue, pale and spotted, translucent and opaque; in mottled schools and on their own.

The fish began to compete with the shadows. Soon tetras flew around a set of water glasses that nestled on our kitchen table, and, oddly, Elise put away the platter made of shadow that had held the plums. Then ghostly blue marlins with a spirited arch to their curve impressed themselves on a window. Sometimes I would look for human faces looking out from behind the fish I made. I knew how they'd be. In my mind's eye I could see their features, and they were soft and ghostly as the fish themselves: comforting, forgiving; suspended in the water that was glass while they floated like moon on water to another place. But still I never found faces in the glass.

Instead, sometimes I would see real ones. Mostly faces Elise had when she came up behind me and showed me her worried but proud reflection. I think she could never decide if she was pleased or displeased by my new interest. And often she appeared half amused, as if she'd merely developed her own private joke about me, some merciful insight that gave her the distance to merely appreciate. The humor that played across her countenance in those moments lightened it in a way I had never seen before.

Other times I saw her face far away on the other side of the glass, settling into itself while she trimmed the lobelia and the roses. Concentration intensified Elise's face. It seemed to become more dense, and opaque; I fancied it was magnetic. In such moments she was most herself.

Once in a while Adam's face would appear next to and slightly above hers: attentive, shy, high-strung, drawn along by some current or scent in the air, all of him rippling like a horse testing the wind before venturing onto a new field. Adam was spending a lot of time with Elise.

But theirs were not the faces I was looking for. I was grateful to them for leaving me. I found a studio set up in the gazebo of a neighbor's house, all windows and grape arbors and paper screens.

Around the same time, I began to lose interest in the shadows. Instead I was beginning to love the brightness, the potential thickness and substance, the very geometry of light itself. As the weather warmed up I left the shadows behind and moved back into the light. In glass, I captured it. I broke off pieces of it and shaped them into glass terrariums, aquariums, pyramids, and orbs; anything that held a world inside it. These were worlds that had always lived within the shadow undisturbed by me, worlds impervious to neglect. And again I found brightly colored glass fish swimming through them from left to right, from back to front, from right to left.

And then one day I willed into being a woman sloping across a sandy floor, supine, calm, curled. There was a white jewel resting on her chest and her hands were raised as if in prayer.

When I was finished with her, I had given Elise that glass woman. She lay at the bottom of an aquarium the size of a brick, with orange angelfish floating around her. Elise treasured her, calling her "Tessie's Mermaid." She cleared a special spot on her dressing table among the clear bottles of perfume and other familiar objects she revered. I would peek in and see necklaces draped over the mermaid in the afternoon to find they had disappeared by evening. This was the mark of Elise's respect, this careful casualness, this absorption of the piece into the details of her daily life. That way she had of stepping back, polishing off the trail of face powder, and then going on again.

◊

But just before Lars's headstone was ready, the mermaid disappeared from the dressing table. When I asked Elise about it early the next morning she smiled and smoothed my hair and told me it was in a good place. That felt like a splash of cold water. But it was also just like her.

I stood in the studio late that afternoon after school was over and felt the shadows and the light gust gently through me.

Then I began to bend the warm metal to my molds and scored it and fired it and felt my mother, Elise, and her ways and how they had helped to slope and curve my life into a shape I had never expected.

When I was very young and Bob had been around, it was all planes and smooth surfaces, fairness and movement. Bob's mysticism was that of a beautifully functioning universe, a place where you learned to ride the currents and to see where they would lead you, all the while relishing yourself, your vitality, your ability to discern what was already there waiting for you. What was your right.

But Elise was a transformer. And transformers do not limit their work to themselves: they transform whoever is around them. Elise's universe was unpredictable, full of hidden forms and depths she tapped as unconsciously as she might pull an unusual implement deep out of a kitchen drawer. Her needs had challenged me as I grew and led me to know glass and light and shadow as deeply and as imperfectly as I knew myself. She had given me what I needed to know to exalt them all.

So it shouldn't have surprised me when she took my offering to her, my gift for all she had challenged me to create, and gave it away. But standing in the studio that day I felt terrible loss.

It was almost dusk and I had stopped to rest while the kiln fired. And through all the pleasant everyday thoughts of glazes and firing times and other young women and what we told each other we did to get by, I heard crooning. It was a familiar but unidentifiable sound. And then I saw Lars crooning to Adam's tetras as he stroked one broad finger across the glass of the aquarium.

I stood up and shook my head. I had the impression I'd been swimming and there was water in it. I thought about the pieces I had done to liberate myself and knew that my pieces had not been mine, or liberating, at all.

And later, when I saw the glass aquarium set into Lars's tombstone, with the light shining through it, em-

bracing the vibrant pigment fish, the clean white ala-
baster nude holding her bright jewel, placed so you
could see right through the stone to another world, to
my other world, I stood steady. It was Adam who
started to cry. And I who silenced him, running my
hands over all his open windows, closing them, like a
mother runs her hands over a sleepless child's eyes.

"Go away, go away, go away," I say now out loud.

"There is no one here but you and me," Luis reminds
me gently.

"And him."

"And him," Luis echoes, looking at me. I can see he's
wondering why I looked not at Javier, but at the clear
laced space between the tent flaps when I spoke.

CHAPTER EIGHTEEN

◇

The first week Javier stays so quiet we are ready to lose him. He spends his waking moments succumbing. His eyes ask for deliverance. But just as desire slips away when you look too hard for it, I see him slipping back to us.

Color begins to light up his skin just as hard earth shades from brown to green in spring. His eyes start to let some of this world in. I can tell he's decided that the harder he fights life the more quickly he'll come back to it, so he's playing possum on it. So I play possum on him, never once letting him know I know what he's up to. I don't want him back any faster than he's ready to come. I think to him, I know when you come back you're going to try to kill me either because I tried to kill you or because I didn't quite kill you. Make sure you get it all sorted out first, because I don't mind de-

fending myself from your convictions but I certainly
don't plan on dying of your confusion.

I watch his progress with all the detachment and at-
tachment and narcissism I feel when I examine my windows alone. I watch the wound turn from purple to
brown to green. His sweats, his silences, his gazes: each
is an event of momentous fascination to me. The tent,
the sky, Luis, the ground. Every day I wake up high.
I'm spurting up inches and shooting down new roots.
I'm always ravenous. And for the first time I understand the desire to stay in the hills indefinitely, to live
this life, to give up the other life and its security and
level peace of mind.

At night I'm filled with harsh dreams. In one a window burns itself into the side of the tent and in it Javier's mother appears. She's wiry and elegant, haloed in
hair that's bleached to a vibrant copper.

"Someone should have done that to him a long time
ago," she informs me. Her voice is sharp, crackling. She
doesn't look at me. "He told me about you," she says.

"I didn't want to spend my life containing him," I
find myself explaining. "I wanted to be able to let down
my guard."

"He would have honored that. He would have made
a softer place for you than anyone. You never told
him."

"He was crazy. Look where he ended up. I know
about that kind of illness, and men."

I can feel her anger swell and harden to match mine.
Her mouth is tightening.

"I was willing you to do it." Now she speaks from
pure wrath. "He's not sick, either. He was pushed too
far and he just gave in to it. And his weakness brought
out yours. I couldn't stand it anymore. I couldn't stand

to see him, the way he suffered. I gave him, I can take him away. I was the one he felt watching him."

"Why didn't you do it yourself?"

"I did. You did."

In the dream we look at each other in astonishment. My anger fades and her face softens. I touch her arm as she touches mine. We are trying to tell each other something, our lips are softly forming words as the window closes and I feel myself crouching into myself and sense the hard ground beneath me, the ragged breath at my elbow, Luis sleeping at my feet.

"No one blames you," Luis interrupts once in the night, resting his hands on my shoulders in the dark.

After that I barely leave the tent. I need him in my sight. My pulse quickens, my nerves quicken, my anger rises like a tidal wave and falls back into itself just before it's ready to break. I know the answer to my own question. He's kept me here to kill him. He set on it, deep inside. And I set myself on trying.

"Keep empty," I tell myself. "Fill up and you fill your life with fear."

Javier comes to when I decide it's time for him to with my flesh wrapped to his flesh. The sun is coming up raucous silver outside the tent. I have hold of his hands and when he begins to clench and unclench them I rise up with the sun at my back and display every ripple, every nuance, every flush of pleasure as it dances and knots my body. On my first stroke, he touches me. His hands remember me. The second time, he opens his eyes. The third time he holds me tightly.

"You're going to be a mess after this, Puig," I say. He feels different. He feels softer, like Adam did, the last time I made love to him.

Adam, who was born-again to commitment and left

us for Nicaragua and a Nicaraguan girl. Adam, who met me in my college studio after he had proposed to the girl. He had gained twenty or thirty pounds and grown a darkish beard that concealed the features of his face. We hadn't seen each other in four years and we knew we wouldn't see each other for several more. His voice was changed. It was braying, hurt, clumsy. After we'd talked for a few minutes he began to strip my clothes off me and I let him.

Partially I let him do it out of amazement that after all that time my body could still be of such burning interest to him. If he needed it that badly, who was I to stop him? And partially I did it out of negligence. What could it matter? After all, we were bound so tight and this was part of the bond. Had always been part of the bond.

First he just wanted to look. I had never felt so looked at. Then he stood me behind a sheet of clear glass taller than I was and felt the glass over my body.

"That's what you want the world to feel like," Adam had said to me, running his hand over the sheet. He touched the part over my left breast and went lower and lower, twirling teasing, blunt, splayed circles that never touched.

I was scared, but I decided to let him play it out. In a way I still believed I was the one who let his father die. Maybe that would be a way of cleansing it. It was worth a shot. I was beholden to him. Then he stripped his clothes off. "No," I said. The way he had me positioned, I couldn't get out from behind the glass unless he moved. I didn't want to push because I was afraid it would break. When he looked at me again his blue eyes were dark. He reached his arms up and spread them apart and braced them against the molding above our heads. Then he began to rock against the glass. "No!" I yelled. He shifted the pressure to his bent knees and reached around, very gingerly, and took me by the waist.

"This is what you want the world to feel like," he mumbled. The edge of the pane was near my neck and I was afraid to move. If I moved he might crash suddenly against the wall and hurt himself. The glass felt cold, and Adam's hands held me like a vise.

"You're fucking crazy," I said.

"You're so good at not breaking it, breaking anything," he said. "Show me how." He was pushing my hips back and forth, pushing himself forward. The sheet was vibrating slightly, beginning to rattle back and forth. "Jesus God," I said, and then it broke with a brilliant cymbal crash into huge curved panes and fell away and we held each other while we bled.

The irony is, the scars on my body look remarkably like leading on a window. They're white scars, raised. Two curved sweeps intersected by an elegant wedge. Not unattractive, objectively. If I look at myself the way I look at a window I please myself. That isn't so much the problem. The problem is explaining how.

Adam's scars were bookends to mine.

Javier was the first man I'd made love with since.

◇

"Hey." Luis is shaking me. "He's better. He wants to see you again."

It's late afternoon. The light is shining yellow in my eyes.

Luis brings his face down close to my face. "It's okay," he tells me. "You'll see."

I walk into the tent. I hear cloth rustle before I see him. And then there he is, sitting up and blinking.

"I scared you bad, huh? I'm surprised you're still here." As he lies back again he whistles softly, as if witnessing a fireworks display.

"I'm surprised you're still here," I reply.

He looks up at the ceiling and takes in the tent, the poles. He says nothing. With his head, he gestures to the cassette player at his side. "You brought her back to us."

"I never dreamed I could stab someone."

"You're a survivor," he says then, as impersonally as he can.

CHAPTER NINETEEN

◇

Here is a dream I never would have imagined I could have dreamed in the long years, the hushed years after the end of Adam, when I studied science in school. The interlude of libraries, calm nights, early dawns, loose camaraderie. The years when the logic of life around me thawed into a logic of order and accomplishment, of thoughtfully distributed power and forward movement. An interlude I didn't think was an interlude but rather the way things would always be from then on. Sanity. Elise's universe vanquished by Bob's. I led myself to emptiness.

I started my way back. I started traveling and ended up in Begar. I helped build the kiln door into a world I once knew. The final spans of Bob's world are snapping or fusing into this world, giving it structure and support. They can no longer hold back dreams like this one.

An important friend of Luis and Javier is getting married in a big white house on a lawn. At the last minute Javier has asked me to join the wedding party. In front of the others, he hands me my dress. It is not an attendant's dress. It is a wedding dress made up of many separate layers that tie and fit over one another in complicated and delicate ways: like banners, like breaths.

There is not much time until the wedding starts. I am shown to an upstairs room of white beds and brass mirrors. I begin to take apart the layers of the dress, and they tangle on the bed, all order lost.

A woman with sparkling black eyes comes in to help me. Together, we untie bows and separate tiny hooks and eyes and lay the pieces out neatly. Other women come in behind us, dress effortlessly, and depart again. The first has Maite's hair. The second has her eyes. The third has her sturdy, graceful arms and her smile. When they walk, their dresses rustle with the chords of slow guitars. When they speak, their voices are the voices that guided me through the field. I feel pulled to the people downstairs, but the task I must complete before I can join them is enormous. From the window, I watch more guests approach the front door. They are an earthy, sophisticated group. I see that they have lived through hardship and I hear triumph in their bawdy jokes and commanding voices. But there is also a lightness to them. They are festive, they are witty, their clothes seem made of gossamer. Gazing out, I know whatever they have been through has settled in a way that's opened new pathways of experience inside them. I can hardly dare to hope I could come to know what they know. I hardly hope to know how they put themselves together.

I put on the first layers of my dress. I can't remember which ones go on in which order, and on top of everything else they seem to be colored and shaped differently from how I've memorized them. It's hard to see how all these different layers, no matter how delicate, will cohere, but I try. I tie on a white sleeveless bodice with a thin linen strip of skirting at each side. Next comes something lacy with frilly sleeves and a black bodice with a train. I wonder at the color, but then that piece, like every other, melds into the next and the next, changing the color and shape of the whole. Even in my frustration I marvel at the genius behind this garment, even though some pieces change color and shape as I touch them. As I work, my shock wanes, my faith in the end result strengthens, and I become certain I will be ready to join the others soon.

Just then, as I crisscross two ribbons down my waist and watch them dissolve into the dress, leaving a sculpted seam in their wake, I hear the wedding begin without me.

I abandon the rest of my task and the room. At the doorway, I look back over my shoulder and what was the diminished pile on the bed appears to have filled with new and enticing textures and shapes. Half dressed, I tiptoe down a back stairway, get into my car, and drive off while a tenor voice intones ceremony behind me. I see I am driving down the street on the hill where I grew up and notice how similar it is to the road that leads to Los Anenomes. I catch a glimpse of the house where Elise and I lived first with Bob and then with Adam and John and Lars. Floating in what was once my bedroom window is a large, pyramid-shaped pane in greens and browns that depicts a hooded figure, a hermit or a monk with Javier's face.

It is then that I discover that there is a new road cut into the earth beyond the house. I turn down it and find that, in my absence, my woods have been mown down. Only the stream still trickles through, steady and calm, gleaming lavender in yellow veldt.

CHAPTER TWENTY

◇

Luis eases the Fiat into second. We follow the road slowly until it breaks through the pine grove and then we're gliding. The sight of the hill moving around me and the road rushing busily along merges with the brisk, almost cleansing pain in my temples.

"You don't have to come," Luis says.

"No. I want to."

He reaches over, fluffs my hair, and grins.

"It's easy now," he tells me.

"One foot in front of the other." I try to speak lightly, to match his tone. It feels good to be moving. I didn't kill anybody. I'm going to buy groceries. Then I'll ride back to the house. This is a pretty okay way to spend a day.

Luis keeps glancing at me. I return the gesture. Soon we're laughing at each other. I gulp down huge draughts of landscape as we drive by, savoring the gentle plain and the hills curling up at the edge of our vision. We turn left at a steep intersection and onto a narrower road twisting high along a dry riverbed and up a hill. Straight ahead, along the horizon, the clouds leave off and the horizon itself turns a smoky blue. A black Ford whizzes by. I start.

Luis begins to hum. It's a song that was popular in the ice cream parlors and discotheques this summer when we knew each other just as faces bobbing in the wake of Javier's bluster.

"The town we are going to," he says, "has quite a large market known for its pretty lace. We'll stop by."

"Los Anenomes could use a little decorating," I agree, quite sincerely. "I had the feeling it was over," I added, changing the subject. "But I was just marshaling my forces, I think." I can almost kill a man and still chat with a friend. The wind coursing past the car strikes me as the very sound of vitality itself.

"*Guapa,*" Luis says. *Pretty one.* "You mustn't ever think that he would say anything to the authorities because he would not. Or intentionally hurt you in any way. Maybe I don't always love him but I know him."

"I know. I think that's all played out now."

The landscape is flattening and widening, and other small roads begin to feed into our own. Each is lightly studded with moving cars. I take my set of car keys out of my pocket and put them on the dashboard.

Luis glances at them. "I remember when I first learned how to drive. I was eleven and Javier taught me on his family's land. I thought, How easy it would be to flick the wheel one way or the other and run into a tree or a little child or a goat or another car. I thought about how close we all live to destruction every day. I wondered, What is it that keeps me from doing such a thing? For weeks I terrified myself. Then gradually I became reassured I would not do such a thing and I stopped worrying. But I wasn't sure that naturally I was not just as capable of the other thing. For years, this slipped my mind. I remembered while we were taking care of him."

The town appears in front of us. I take in each detail with excitement, it's like I'm seeing a small European village for the first time.

"Nervous?" Luis asks.

"No. Why? Do I look nervous?"

"Yes."

I don't answer.

"It's natural," he reminds me.

The village is neatly devoid of modern buildings and clutter. It's ordered around a stark promontory and protected on the steep side with a wall. The outermost rim of dark stone housefronts looks resined with the soft decay of another age. I anticipate the small luxuries of a stand-up bar with an espresso machine, plates of deep-red peppers and plump golden omelettes on the bar, even the rack of fifty-peseta potato-chip bags on a side wall. I think of the lone telephone booth this village is sure to have and of the *casa de huéspedes,* where I could nap on a bed in a private room I locked myself, with an old-fashioned key. I can almost see the matrons who'll eye me with benign disapproval as I sit in their square with my worn jeans and my scruffy boots, fan out my tousled hair, and brood in the sunlight in a way that to them means trouble.

Then, the thought of these small pleasures fills me with inexplicable sadness. There's no longer the congruence there once was between them and me. Enjoying them won't reassure me of who I am or even of what pleasure is. Not the way it used to.

"When I come here I sometimes buy a newspaper," Luis confides as we pull into a parking place on a narrow street, "and sit at the bar in the market and have a cognac. I like the lace. I like the way it hangs."

"No girls?"

He shakes his head and sticks out his chin.

We walk up the narrow sidewalk past windows tidily cluttered with the latest in kitchen appliances: squat, funny items in strange acid colors that look as though they'll never quite achieve their purpose, but also as though those who buy and sell them assume that nothing quite ever will. We pass a jeweler, and then a grocer with cartons of vegetables that burst untidily onto the street. I can hear running water.

"Civilization," I say, laughing. Up ahead the road widens the way roads like this do on their way to marketplaces. Women hurry past us, carrying woven shopping bags and guiding sharp metal carts.

I'd love to bring Elise one of my favorite winter fruits, a cherimoya, if I could only get it past customs. There is no way of telling when the day I pass customs will come, but I know now it will. To my delight, I spy a carton of them; while I have been at Los Anenomes fall has come. I lean over and pick up one of the soft, lumpy green fruits, thinking of the sweet snow-drift of flesh inside and of the glossy black seeds plunged deep in its center. I feel almost drunk as I lean down to inhale the fragrance of the entire bin. A clerk flaps slowly toward me. Luis grabs my elbow and we lunge forward together. "Come on," he hisses. "Don't draw attention."

"I'm just so happy . . ."

"Please," he says. "Be delicate."

"I didn't seduce you," I say, changing the subject.

"No, no," he says impatiently. "I was the one who did the seducing. The pharmacy is down to the left. It'll take me about half an hour to pick up what we need. Here's your village," he says affectionately. He sweeps his arm outwards. "Enjoy."

And there he leaves me.

The wind gusts around me. I stand alone a moment in the cold. It feels good. We're in the mountains now, after all. I can't remember having felt hot or cold for a long time. Los Anenomes is not a place of temperature: there the play of light and shadow eclipse the play of other senses. There light and shadow and creature comforts like warmth and the taste of good food seem mutually exclusive.

I walk in a circle and stamp my feet. I breathe out hard to see if my breath shows white. It doesn't. Two passing women eye me curiously. They are wearing light sweaters, whereas I'm shivering in my heavier jacket.

I have my half hour. I suppose I could have more if I request it, but I'm grateful for Luis's friendly authority. I decide that later I'll return and browse through the newspaper kiosk and maybe go to see the lace. But first I'll walk to the wall at the end of the village.

I stumble quickly along the sidewalk. It's late morning and the street is almost entirely populated with women, old men, and small children. There's none of the slow, majestic, human gathering inward toward the square that I know will begin at the end of the day. Instead, villagers scatter like handfuls of marbles up alleys and around corners. As I move upwards and away from them thick puffs of exhaust from a car with out-of-province plates crowd my path. A family snaps out of the car and heads toward the marketplace. A hazel-eyed toddler in a gold paper crown regards me from the shelter of a doorway. I want to get where I'm going. I begin to jog along. The sidewalk widens, the shops thin out, then accede to the wall behind them. The sky is blue-white and mottled with gray shadows, a high canopy of a sky; I've finally found the cathedral ceiling of the world, and the canopy of bright blue I faced most days is just a makeshift tent.

I slow down again. When I've almost reached the wall I stop walking, turn back, and face into the wind to feel the multiplicity and lightness of the forest that cooled and nourished me when I was a child. I see Elise arranging the full, fragrant bundle of peonies in Adam's arms the summer after Lars's death, and I remember Adam cradling them as if they were as heavy and precious as a child. I see a flock of tiny black glass birds I tempered in the kiln in Begar. And I remember the water pouring over me in the shower at Los Anenomes.

At this moment I feel as clear and neutral as that water. But I also know a knife blade has fallen into that clear stillness of mine and keeps on going, deep, deep, sinking as surely as if a godly hand were driving it toward my source. But as I realize this I feel the blade vanish, its sharpness and weight absorbed into aqueous clarity. And I'm left as fresh and alert as if I'd walked for miles instead of a few village blocks.

I climb the stairs to the top of the wall. The lenses of three viewfinders on antique stands sweep out across the countryside. The metal feels cold. I put in a coin and peer through. Far out in front of me is the foggy tangle of the coast. In between stretch the ice-green plains. Out of habit I study the roads running through them and the salient features of the hamlets, checking to see if any speak to me. That's how I landed in Begar to begin with.

I pick out a dusky road that bleeds off the highway, makes a wide, twisting crook, and ends in a collection of buildings as white as the sun and clean as morning. One looks official, a city hall or a school, and another appears to be a long, rambling home built onto again and again over the years. There are a few small store-fronts and shacks and the requisite fresh white chapel. Beyond the house I imagine a paddock of horses. Then, as if to chide my fantasy, an old man herds a knot of shaggy goats around the house with a stick.

I contemplate stepping out of a car on the swept steps of that graciously officious central building. I thank the driver who's picked me up hitchhiking, a maternal woman who approves of my fearlessness and disap-proves of what I've made of it. After walking through the cool, tiled interior of the building (which will turn out to be a museum for indigenous arts), I spend the siesta in a little cafe on a side street, nothing but light and wind in my head. It would be easy to stay over-night in that town, to watch the swallows swirl around the bell tower as dusk falls. When I'd listened long enough to the music of the stars I would fall asleep. Wake up, pay my bill, and go home. Go home? Go home where?

I can't explain what I was doing at Los Anenomes with the two of them. Why Los Anenomes was the place I started really working again.

I turn around and look back over the town.

It's musty. Most small villages look best from above, all roofs and calm and clarity, even when you know there may be nothing but close-mindedness and dashed

dreams underneath. But this village makes me uneasy.
For a moment I savor the anachronism of my presence
here. Beyond, I can see the autumn-turned land dipping
down and the roads dipping with it. In the blur of distant hills lies Los Anenomes, and Javier.

Two teenaged boys in black start climbing up the
stairs to the top of the wall and I start down, pulling
my jacket in tightly around me and listening to the sharp
tap of my own footsteps.

I don't know how long I've been up there. I never
wear a watch and the church-tower clock registers the
same time as it did on my way up. The walk into town
feels longer than the walk out and the chill I initially
welcomed is starting to settle in my bones. In the ki-
osks, local headlines chatter of a regional squabble over
agricultural exports. I'm looking for something that will
shed some perspective, snap me back into the world,
but the only international press to be found is a selection of French magazines for homemakers. I stand in
front of the kiosk for a long time anyway. Time's passing by. It's been more than a month now since I've been
nowhere. I have to find my place again.

I take the road that should lead to the market. A bus
pulls up at the corner. Inside are three old men. Two
older woman and a young mother and child join them.
I can get on the bus, get off, and dial Carmen or Marisol
from a phone booth. Even Elise. I can open the door to
my apartment in Begar and just stand there, taking in
the round table and the apricot runner, the slightly
swaybacked daybed with the rose print swooning
against one wall. I could take in the perfect, slightly
absorbent serenity of that room. It had been a wonderful place to sleep, to think up my goblets and birds and
lamps, and heal. I had spent hours just lying on that

daybed, like a little child, while the shadows went from brown to green and the swallows began to rise for their slow evening circle. There was a tangle of gorged, artful blossoms outside one window, and as dusk fell they always seemed to come erect and enlarge against the gathering darkness. And for a few magical moments their glory would intensify and triumph against the world of the dying sun. They'd seem so close then, almost menacingly so. And I would just lie there, their prisoner, until the moment was done. And the emptiness that came next would fill me up and free me to roam like a wind through the darkness.

No one knew I was free and roaming. As far as the rest were concerned, I was just a foreign woman with money of her own. Later, after the nights on the beach or after the dancing, I would turn alone to that spacious, slightly muffled sitting room of mine and let it sap off the vestiges of my spent wanderlust.

Magic. The ions in that room had their own special charge. I told Elise about it in one of my occasional letters. She was the only one I thought might understand. She never commented.

It hasn't been quite a month. The rent was just due. It might still be there, waiting for me.

I find myself thinking of the freshly cut yellow flowers my landlady always left for me in the blue vase in the center of the table where I read and ate. I think of my books, and of an antique piano shawl Elise sent me from Paris, and about a few pieces of clothing whose weight and smell still create home.

I still know exactly how. How to get on the bus, to travel, to pick up the phone, to be in the apartment, to sit in that wonderful shielded space. To decide what direction to take next, and to take it. But I can't make the pieces quite fit together that would get me there and I turn away.

I want to get back to the windows. I want to render the look of that sky before it disperses. I have nothing to *do* in this village and it isn't the kind of place you go to if you don't have anything to do. I still don't know what time it is, but I wish Luis would hurry. I turn toward the street that ends in the marketplace.

◇

The market is a tin-roofed cavern, disproportionately large for such a small town. Sound rumbles from one end to the other. The air is full with the scent of life and brisk business, and in the cupolas of high darkness the edges of a few banners of white lace are visible. As always, it feels damper inside; keener, safer, as if the place had its own sealed climate which sheds a special kind of dew. I inhale the fragrance of new sawdust on the floor and run my feet through.

It must be between eleven and twelve, judging by the level of noise and bustle. I am in the butchers' section. Orderly queues of women snake from side to side of gleaming stands laden with hams and sausages. *"Quién es la última,* who is last in line?" I hear one woman murmur, and then another, and another. *"I am, I am, I am,"* come the echoes and obediently the newcomers line up behind the old. Before me, an almond-haired matron with gold hoop earrings and overtended brown leather pumps tastes a slice of smoked pork. Farther in, I can see the edge of a cascade of beet greens stained golden by a shard of light. I want to taste, to touch. A man lurches into my right shoulder. *"Despistada,"* he mumbles sharply, *"watch where you're going."* It's true. I'm in the way. I retreat to the side of the entrance and then out the door.

Blinking in the sunlight, I walk down the arcade of shops that go down the long side of the marketplace. Pyramids of eggs and stacks of plaid plastic baskets fight for my attention. There's the bracing icy smell of fresh fish, and the jewel-toned feathers of trussed game birds glow high in the dark eaves. I feel so disoriented by, yet so satisfied with this sensory barrage that I stop and look everywhere, a child in a candy shop. I've always been too self-conscious to be a gawker. And the side arcades of markets have always revolted me: I've always avoided them, and now I'm reveling in one.

I'm very hungry. I can't remember the last time I was actually hungry. I rustle and probe and push through the stands looking for the perfect morsel. Vendors watch me. The local yogurt will be sickly sweet. I don't have the patience to queue for meat, and fruit is far away inside. Finally a row of sugar-encrusted, golden magdalenas catches my attention: so round, so dense, so comforting. I imagine one, two, seven, melting in my mouth and filling me up.

Soon I'm digging in my bag for the pastries, I'm disposing of them like gumdrops. I don't know or care if I'll meet Luis as planned. I decide it will happen eventually anyway: the town isn't large enough for us to miss each other and I'm sure he'll never abandon me.

Overhead the sky is brightening but the air stays crisp and heavy. I walk to the back plaza of the marketplace. In front of me, beyond a low wall at the end of an asphalt plaza, the mountain flows downward. Above, their backs to the sky, vendors sell potatoes, yellow squash, and honey.

"*Oye, reina*" calls a cheerful male voice behind me.

Reina, queen, I've always envied the way the Spanish speak it to each other in supportive irony; it's one of the endearments most likely to float after a girl in stiletto heels shouldering a basket of groceries on a busy street, among the least likely to be tossed to a foreign woman who seems to need no one. It's a special password in a secret language, and for the first time it's being directed at me.

I whirl around, willingly disarmed, to greet Luis. Instead, I see a large woman in a print dress with a wide, lively face and two blond braids pinned around her head. She looks familiar.

"Sorry, did I surprise you? Miriam Harkin," she continues in what is not a male voice but contralto, extending her hand. "From Castelldelféls. And Oakland. I came to that kiln-raising the other month, remember?"

"Of course. Author of fabulous fried chicken. Fried chicken and tortilla española, wasn't it?"

"You guys get that thing working right?" She peers at me and shuffles a threadbare green canvas shopping bag from one hip to the other hip. "I told Evan, was he sure about the hookup."

"Fine. Works great."

"I was just thinking about you the other day. I saw some of your stuff in a shop while I was making a call and I said to myself, I guess it's still working. Evan isn't there anymore," she explains.

"Yeah, actually I haven't been around much lately. But we really appreciated your help. This summer's been . . ."

"I know, I know." Kindly and impatiently, the rest of my apology is shaken off. Miriam squints at me again, the eyes bright-blue chips under the shade of her hand. She shifts the bag back to the other hip, and I notice it's straining with the weight of smaller packages inside. "Gee, I can tell the sun is bothering you. Want to get a drink?"

We enter the market's back door, near the lace vendors. Cross-sections of white gossamer drift through the darkness; soft, transparent, clearly articulated. So simple they can't be broken down further, but complex enough to please for a long time, they strike me as the blueprint for something good. I feel light-headed. Miriam is asking me which shops have nice buyers and which don't and whether I've seen her husband's entry in a certain gallery show, which she thinks has been poorly curated. Meanwhile I can't take my eyes off the ceiling of floating lace.

"Yeah, you can make some beautiful curtains from that." Miriam patiently makes her way down the aisle with her heavy load. "My neighbor had one, a whole scene of stars at night. Pretty. Hey, here we are."

I order coffee and she a Coke.

"Now, tell me, what are you doing these days?" She settles her bag on the floor and smooths out her skirt.

"Well, I don't know exactly how to answer that."

The bright eyes soften slightly. For the first time, I notice her take in details of my appearance. Her eyes settle on my hair, my hands, my shoes.

"We had a fine time of it," Miriam says, taking the paper off her straw. "Our first year here we had no hot water all winter. Heater went, and we couldn't afford to replace it. Anyway, that's a long time ago. This life's good, you know. And you can show—anywhere." She starts ticking off fingers. "London, Paris, Madrid, Ibiza . . ."

"How long have you been here?" One part of me speaks. Another scouts for Luis. A third watches the lace.

"Oh gosh, ten years now. First I was engaged to a local fella, then I went home, then back with Evan."

I turn and take her in fully: beneath the Wagnerian braids, a faded rose-and-turquoise dress whose skirt is loose and full; a harlequin brooch and matching earrings carefully selected from the best the Sunday street vendors have to offer. The short nails are a neat, vivid pink. I recognize the leather belt as a type I've noticed in the window of a fashionable but inexpensive Barcelona boutique.

When I first joined the studio and fell in briefly with the expatriate crowd, it amused me to see these careful European details reinterpreted in ways that were so completely American. But then, the bag and the braids and the jewelry would look just as out of place back home as they do here. From the next stool, Miriam is being eyed by a young Spanish matron in a brown plaid skirt and a conservative leather blazer, but Miriam pays no attention. Comfortably, consciously wrinkled, she leans back on her stool and sips the Coke. The thought of the eyebrows she must raise walking through the slim lines and smooth veneers of the Barcelona shopping galleries makes me grin.

Then, I'm wistful. I can't remember being recognizable to much of anyone but Javier and Luis. I won't be easily understood. I'm leaded together out of too many pieces.

"I've seen girls get in trouble here," Miriam says, apropos of nothing.

"Really?" I'm more interested than she knows.

Solemn, her eyes run over my face and hands again. "But when I met you I knew you could handle yourself. So did Evan. I can tell you're not one of them."

She sips on her soda.

"Sometimes you hit a few rough spots. But a lot of water goes under that bridge."

Just then I see Luis is waiting for me at the corner of a lace stand in the second aisle. We make eye contact. With a long, unhurried, fluid movement, he lights a match on a matchbook cupped in one hand and, examining a piece of lacework above his head, touches the flame to his cigarette. He stamps the match out under his foot, looks at me, and nods toward the piece that has caught his attention. It has an interesting border, a pattern of white bows aflutter like moths near light. Here and there among the bows are slender needles, whose white threads spin and weave and drift into the fabric's center. There I see a stylized letter T. I have to look carefully to see it. It's buried beneath a curtain of soft detail. But it's there.

"You guys have any more time to rent out at your studio? I know a couple guys who were looking, oh, last month. They might have found something, I don't know. But you guys have a good setup."

"Maybe. I don't know. Tell them to come by in a few weeks and I'll see."

"Just asking."

I spot Luis again, who is now talking quietly to the woman at the lace stall.

I wonder if I'll even be there through the fall. So many of the people I met in Begar live from small comfort to small comfort, like candles lighting their way through a vast darkness. It's been nice to shelter myself from that darkness for a while. But once you know that place, your eye adjusts. You know the place isn't dark at all, it's as pale and limitless as the sky. You can see the light circles are actually part of it. They are like the pattern in lace, or leading on a pane. What they bracket out is the same as what they bracket in. "Miriam," I ask, stirring the last half inch of my coffee with the little espresso spoon, "do you have many friends here?"

The eyes crinkle, the earrings swing, and she looks up over the bar. "Lot of acquaintances. Few friends. But that's the price you pay—"

"For doing what the hell you want."

I can feel Luis like distant sunlight at my left side.

"Ehh," Miriam says, uttering the universal expression of contented resignation. Her eyes are still smiling but her mouth is sad.

"Yeah. I know what you mean."

"Gotta go, kiddo. Don't be a stranger."

" 'Bye."

It's only after she's gone that it occurs to me neither of us has asked the other what she's doing at Las Areyas.

I get up and pay the bill. Luis approaches me holding the lace piece with the T at its center in one hand. As he comes closer I feel like a huge sail filling with an enormous wind. Now that I have the wind I can turn in any direction and move. I plant my feet in the ground as he smiles his shy smile and bears down on me.

PART III

RIVER
OF
GLASS

CHAPTER TWENTY-ONE

◇

Luis understands right away. I always assume that leaving a place or people will take longer than it does. But almost as soon as I describe my plan the Fiat is moving away from the marketplace and toward the highway. He doesn't even want me to explain to Javier. "Better for you this way" is his only comment, and I wonder if he thinks that seeing Javier would make me lose my resolve.

Meanwhile, I want him to understand why I have to go. I want someone to understand how I need to be myself, how I crave the space to keep the threads of images forming. I'm not sure he hears me, though. His eyes keep traveling. After about an hour, the car stops.

Luis walks around to my side and opens the door. We're parked in front of a gas station on the highway. The road signs tell me we're close to the coast, about an hour south of Begar.

"You can get a bus from here."

My heart begins pounding.

A quick kiss on each cheek. "I'll see you," Luis says.

As the Fiat pulls onto the northbound ramp Luis turns and waves. Then he changes lanes and I lose sight of him.

◇

At Begar, only two or three of us get off the bus; summer's gone. Walking quickly and hoping no one I know sees me, I head through town for the breakwater, where I watch the sunset.

When it's dark, I walk down to the edge of the water and let its movement polish me. I pick up handfuls of sand. It's damp and pleasantly granular, like the pie crusts Elise and I used to make together when I was young. Our heads bent and silent, we'd gaze through the wide windows into the garden while the sound and sway of plant life seemed to rush around us, its rhythm ringing in change even as the elastic substance in our hands promised continuity.

It's more than a year now since I lay in the hospital bed, firing the pattern Adam's breaking glass had leaded on my skin, firing it good and hard and solid with healing. That's when I finally told Elise about me and her stepson. And I told her the truth, although I didn't have to.

She listened to me with the gravity of a monk. Briefly, from within the haze of drugs, I swore I saw her forehead elongate, her skin gray with compassion and restraint, her fingers touch each other in the shape of a house of prayer. And then she surprised me.

"Passion," she said softly, "does things like that. We all fall down and pick ourselves up again—that's the art of life. But doing that makes you keen. It makes you want to live. That's all. You're just a grown-up." Then she laughed the light, pealing laugh. But it was gentler than usual.

As she left she stopped at the door and laid her forehead against the frame. For a moment she just stood there watching the stealthy shadows of nurses in the hallway. And then she said, "I think your stepfather did what he did because he stopped living out of passion. He was trying to live from other things. The other way would have kept him around for a long while no matter how ugly it got. Sometimes you need ugly." Then she left, briskly.

Now I wade into the water and the cold makes my toes tingle.

◇

It isn't even midnight when I begin loading, by candlelight, my studio things into a rental car. A note at the apartment has warned me that everyone has left the studio with the warm weather: the power has been shut off. I pick up scraps of the shiny brown wrapping paper I use to sketch and plot and cartoon, relishing the sound and feel of it in my hands. I fill a small suitcase with it. Next it's time to clean tools and dust the sharp T-square. I arrange brushes neatly in jars, crisp and as full of possibility as new pencils on the first day of school. The set of panes I was working on before everything happened is stacked up against one wall. Odd, what I'd painted on them, experimenting: a child of smoke looking into an empty room. Some soldiers. Two figures rocking together, clutching a sharp crescent in their hands that could be a moon or a knife. Even in the dark, they seem to glow thick and soft as lake ice. But they're just on the way. They're not quite right.

It's time.

I am humming the Ode to Joy. So corny.

I pull the little red fire ax from its rack. I test its weight in my hands. I keep on whistling. *Remember it once more, and forget forever.*

When I'm ready, the ax flies forward. It keeps on going, through the stack of panes, through the wall, and the wind rushes and curls in. Gracefully, neat as precision dancers, the glass slivers corkscrew into the air as if this was the moment they were made for.

CHAPTER TWENTY-TWO
◇

I drive north, navigating the thread of new images that is running continuously now. A man's chin and diamond earring. A woman in a high window, throwing gold. Coins with transparent centers. Flowers, houses, bolts of lightning, aprons, chairs, the shadow of a prow—all moving helter-skelter through a current of what could be water or air.

The thread runs out a few days later at dawn, and I pull off the road to sleep: this morning unlike other mornings I'm too foggy to stick it out until a town and a pension. Almost immediately, I dream. I am in the main room of a house with a roof of arches and bones. Draped over frames on a wooden table, white strips of cloth billow and sail and I paint them while Luis and Javier stand by.

◇

In this dream I have never painted anything before. Flowers and abstracts float on pale backgrounds. It's magical. I become more and more confident. I spy a blank surface, high under the eaves of the eastern wall. I reach high, high, twice my height, and by guiding my hands toward the whiteness more color seems to appear. On the canvas, flowers spatter and spin.

Through the long row of windows on the northern wall, I behold a procession of burning torches that are threading slowly toward me and the two Argentines over a far hill. I understand that they are coming for me: what I am doing is forbidden. To protect me, the men wrap me in one of my own white sheets. But before they can finish, the torchbearers close in. I prepare to surrender. Suddenly, the procession kneels. The faces fill with shyness and longing. The torches become lighted matches held in offering. The world goes silent except for the tiny, hopeful hiss of flames.

I freeze, incredulous. And then I laugh.

"It's not that important," I tell them.

I turn to the southern windows and find a harbor opening into a violet sea. The sky is studded with stars that gather in strange and wonderful constellations brighter than any I have ever seen. Below them, a sailboat crosses the mouth of the harbor. On deck I can make out a blond woman, adjusting ropes and gears, who wears one of the stars in her ear.

◊

I wake up, remember the dream, look at where I am, and start to laugh. I chuckle all the way to the nearest good hotel, where I check in, take a long bath, and consume paella for two, since individual servings are not available.

After lunch, I go to *telefónicas* and hand the operator

a list of three phone numbers on two continents. I call a Canadian photographer I met last year in the south of France, Bob, and Elise.

"Describe something where you are so I know what it looks like," Elise orders, the closest she'll dare to inquiring after my well-being in this phone call. So I look out the window and relay every detail of the sixteenth-century church across the street, down to the last ornamental sculpture, a seashell. For good measure, I throw in the Aston Martin with British plates parked in front of the church, the pots of orange and pink geraniums on the sidewalk, and the lizard that's crawling up the nearest of them.

"That's nice," she sighs, relieved.

I stay overnight in this town; no dreams, no thoughts. In the morning I have a new direction.

CHAPTER TWENTY-THREE

◇

There is a certain beauty to the moment a window crumples in on itself and its fragments sift to the floor. I'm only sorry I won't be here in the morning to see it. The cool night air blows on my face and all four directions beckon.

"Turn around where I can see you," says Luis's voice from inside Los Anenomes.

"Do you have a flashlight?" I run toward him.

"Maite?" he asks.

"Tess. Just Tess." I think, I hope that's good enough.

"Tessie." He sounds curious, entertained. Not angry at all.

"I'll make you more. I promise. Just stand back."

There are ways to tap the glass so it falls quick and

straight, a waterfall. And if I tap it another way, it shivers and falls softly into itself. Glass sprays pools on the ground. Soon I hear heavy, solid footsteps, and a golden flashlight beam lights the drifts in brilliant detail.

"I think this calls for the cognac," Javier says to Luis.

"I'm leaving," I explain into the darkness. "Actually, I already left. I turned around. I had to say goodbye."

I turn my flashlight on him. Javier looks sleepy and surprised. Behind him I see the window of the room where he and I slept that first night. For the first time I notice how in the couple of weeks since he's recovered it's become a real bedroom: four-poster with spread, washstand, night table, chair, rug. A hurricane lamp on the night table, not one of mine, is lit low, and an open book lies at its side.

Javier leans against the side of the house and looks up at the stars. "Funny way to say goodbye."

"It's something I have to do. I can't explain. I just have to."

"I see." There is a pause. "Come on," he says finally. "Come inside and have a drink."

As he pours cognac into the glasses, he croons to a bird that has begun to warble outside. Dawn has just broken. I look outside and notice that the sailboat is gone.

"She's in dry dock." Luis follows my gaze. "Daniel's getting out. She was always for him. She's *Planetario II.*"

"That's good," I say. "I heard in town they auctioned off *Planetario.*"

Javier nods and hands me my glass. "We're on our way out, too. Danny's ferrying her around to Galicia and we're going to meet him there."

I swirl the brandy in my glass.

"So. You have everything you need."

"Our ship came in." He grinned. "So to speak. A few days after you left. We've done enough. It's the right time. We're going home soon."

"Galicia. That's above Portugal, isn't it? Where the pilgrims go, Santiago?"

"Yes. Santiago. We stay near there for a while and then we sail down to Canárias and go across from there since . . ."

"I was thinking about going to Portugal next."

"You? Why?"

"To see Coimbra. And the Atlantic. It's been a long time since I've seen the Atlantic. You know, you've got a print of Coimbra upstairs."

My plan has been to go back to Elise's boat after Portugal and find a way to settle into my work.

As Javier suggests, "We could give you a ride," I have already started to say, "So I'm guessing I'm going to be tailing you."

"As far as the coast. You can come with us as long as you stop doing that." Javier nods toward the broken window. "My mother holds the deed to this place. Leave my mother a window, Tessa, why don't you?" And he walks off in the other direction.

◇

Before we leave, I drive my car around to where the jagged windows are and take one of the boxes and a shovel from the trunk and dig a hole. When the hole is deep enough, I climb into the house through a broken window and plunge the shovel just once into the river of glass that flows at the bottom of the wall. I climb back out, and bury all that richness in the ground.

Inside the box I've taken from my car are slivers of glass from the Begar studio. Very carefully, with my bare hands, I scoop a handful of them into the hole I've made and cover it over with silt. I dip the shovel back into the pile inside the parlor window at Los Anenomes and replenish the box with them. Then I move this carton to the white Fiat, along with every- thing else.

CHAPTER TWENTY-FOUR

◇

Javier tells stories as he drives from Los Anenomes across his adopted country to the coast. All the kilometers passing under his feet loosen him up in a way they hadn't when we used to take to the road.

By the time Luis joins in two hundred kilometers later, eyes have been gouged, cattle have been stolen, and women have exposed their breasts at formal dinners for prominent families. Now Javier switches on the car radio, ostensibly to keep us up to date on the weather and roads, but really, I suspect, to remind himself where he is while his stories spread out over the world.

By then it's dark. We leave the soft hills of the east and start to wind through the tough verdure of the central highlands. We've already picked the little town on the northern coast where we'll split up and I'll go north and they'll go west, and home. Every once in a while, we swing around a bend and the headlights loop over a thick copse of evergreens. On the radio, a gentleman with a sonorous voice and dancing vowels reviews an art exhibit in the Canary Islands. I open the window a crack so the wind will dance across my face.

By the time a white dawn is breaking, we're in the dusty brown center of the country and Luis is driving. Snow-cuffed plains roll out in every direction. I feel both solitude and companionship. A power plant springs up from the earth. Wires and scaffolds lace up the sky, then set it free. In the distance, a sharp black bell in an open tower slices the sky in two. The Spaniards understand a skyline. Everywhere, towers are showing off the sky the way a necklace shows off décolletage.

"Thinking up more ways to get us in trouble with those creations of yours?" Javier teases.

I smile. "How can you tell?"

Now he smiles.

"You're as transparent as they are. You get a look on your face. Don't worry, it's an interesting look."

He puts a tape in the cassette player, and the familiar guitar music and male voices fill the car.

I groan. "Not more of that. Turn on the radio again, okay?"

Another smile. "Ah. But this is a tape you have not heard."

I listen. Songs play. They are replaced by a murmur. Among the voices a couple of guitars begin to play. People sing. I can't make out the words; the sound is muddy. But it's clear these are the sorts of songs sung in the dark, around a campfire. I hear something familiar.

"Is that you singing?" I ask Javier.

He nods. "And some others."

Just then, a deep laugh soars through the car. It isn't mine, but the voice is a woman's.

"There it is." Luis smiles.

"Maite," Javier explains, as if this were obvious and something everyone should know. "Listen, listen . . ." And then the voice laughs again.

"What in heaven's name was she laughing at?" I ask. Low-pitched and mellow, the sound is entirely without self-consciousness. It's the sound of a person enjoying life fully.

Javier shrugs. "I don't know. She wasn't talking to either of us at the time. She was fiddling with this little thing." He swats the cassette player.

"Maybe it was your singing, *jefe.*"

"Where were you?" I ask.

"We had a party after a demonstration. About a month before we ended up camping for good, and not far away. Very fastidious, Luis's sister. She taped everything."

Low voices, whispers, and chuckles weave through night sounds in the out-of-doors. There is a creak.

"The hammock," explains Luis.

And there it is again, but softer. Maite laughing. Then the sound becomes muffled, as though she were hiding her face in a coat or a pillow.

"She wasn't supposed to do that up there," Luis explains. "Laugh or tape."

And while the tape plays, the men beam, I relax in the company of another woman's energy, and the four of us ride together.

When it ends I turn on the radio. Two poets are describing the fertile expanse that was America to the spatially unenlightened of Europe. Javier listens for a minute. Then he drowns out the interview with a story about an ill-fated smugglers' convention in Antarctica.

It is time for me to chime in.

Near Portland, Maine, I venture, an ocean siren with seaglass for eyes, nipples, and navel makes love to a lobsterman. The next trap the man hoists to the surface contains crustaceans laced with semiprecious stones and real coral instead of roe. The lobsterman gives the first to his mother, who has never touched a lobster. She devours every bit unknowingly, and becomes as dependent upon her son's catch as an addict is on his drug.

"That's a good one," says Luis.

In Denmark, I try, a baker commits suicide after finding his son and daughter in an incestuous position among the flour sacks. The son, who has decided never to forgive his father for his suicide, sets up a rival bakery in revenge, which supplies all the best brothels in the provinces. Meanwhile, the penitent daughter makes four thousand loaves of bread a day for the rest of her life and casts every last one into the North Sea, where they turn into silver fishes and swim away.

I fall silent, thinking of the window of Maite and Adam, which was one of the first I smashed.

In Belfast, says Javier, a curious young Protestant woman follows a Catholic priest to a sacred shrine where he secretly nurses fallen rebels. Later, he comes upon her hiding place by chance.

"Oh, sure, he just happens to trip over her," Luis complains.

"Life is like that," I defend.

Javier goes on. Both peacelovers at heart, the two fall in love. When their child is born, its cries are heard by men searching for the girl. While the priest fends the men off, the girl holds a pillow to the child's mouth so it will not betray them. She removes the pillow before the child asphyxiates, but not before the blood supply to its extremities is cut off, and a foot must be amputated. Full of remorse, they flee and the priest and the girl die young. But the disabled child grows up wise and resilient beyond his years, and is destined to govern and unify their country.

"I'm not dying young," I say to Javier. "Speak for yourself."

"It's just a story," he counters defensively.

It's my turn again: In the North American plains in the nineteenth century, a lonely and loving brother and sister decide to make love to each other on either side of a ground-floor window. They have always been able to touch snowflakes that way without melting them, so they rationalize that this method is one that offers a certain immunity.

"I can't say what happens next," I say.

"Oh, yes you can," says Luis offhandedly, swatting a fly off his ear.

"If you don't," says Javier, "you lose and we get to decide the loser's prize."

I groan. Bitten brown fields flash by outside me.

I plunge on: Unaware of what could happen, their slow and delicate desire builds until they are compelled to push out the bottom of the window, which moves as easily as a cloud. But that isn't enough. They want their mouths and cheeks and chests to meet. Emboldened, they smash the glass away with their torsos, fall to the ground, and consummate their act, scarred for life. In later years, as the scars fade to white, the feathery outlines that are their residue have the shape of perfect snowflakes.

Snow begins to spatter the windshield and the fields and all three of us fall silent.

Javier throws a surreptitious glance at the faint white scar that peeks out at my neck. He turns up the radio.

"I can tell you one about a guy who tried to save his sister and led her murderers to her instead," Luis obliges.

"And I can tell you one about a fellow who tried to try and save the world but led his beloved and many others to their deaths," adds Javier. "And," he goes on, "gave his beloved's brother the idea he'd done it, too."

In the rearview mirror, I look at Luis, who's blinking in the backseat. He shakes his head and blows air out from between his teeth as if he's finally finished a really hard job.

"Well," I say, "I could tell you a story about a man who died." It's Lars I have in mind, but I'm not really interested in telling that story. I just want to show a little solidarity for Luis.

"Boring," says Javier. "All men die."

He opens a package of crackers with his teeth and offers me one.

I twirl the radio dial. Symphonic overtures. Viennese waltzes. Mambas. Songs of requited love, unrequited love, faded love, secret love, conjugal love, civic love, proud love, static. More static. I keep on turning. Once in a while Luis or Javier asks me for a map. Meanwhile, I recall this country in springtime and plot how to stylize the small, flamelike flowers in glass and line. I keep planning how to put down all the new images I see. And, how, after a good French dinner, I am going to sleep in a barge on top of the tides. Towns go by.

"We're getting there," says Luis, as we turn onto the mountain road to the northern coast where the green fields grow almost to the edge of the sea, and where our journey together ends. The floor of the tavern in this town, where we stop for lunch, is cushioned with sawdust, and the cider that runs almost as plentifully as seawater bubbles and foams with air. On our way out, it begins to rain lightly.

Javier decides to rent us a house for the night. We dine together, smiling in silence. Everyone's far away. Later, I settle down on a bare mattress and watch the water sheet and dance down the glass. Behind me, the men wander around the empty, damp-edged rooms, afraid to leave yet dubious about sitting down on the cold ground. Finally they settle for playing cards on the black Windsor bench that is the only piece of furniture in the living room.

By morning, the rain has stopped. The air is very quiet and charged, the way air is when it's snowing. Outside, the sea is bluer than it has been and it ripples toward me in crests as dainty as the collar of a baby's dress. Flags snap in the wind. Far out in the bay, two hunched men in brown caps row a dinghy cross-current.

It's very early. Javier and Luis haven't yet stirred. I walk outside where the breeze smells of running water and the ground springs back under my feet and open the trunk of the car.

All I need is one more piece. The first one I see happens to be blue and almost triangular, like the Sky Tooth. I put it in my pocket and go back to the house. I wish I had an address to leave them, but I don't. I watch them sleep for a while. I might see them someday anyway. On a piece of paper, I write *Goodbye and good luck.* I weigh down the note with the blue glass, and leave it in a place where they will be sure to find it. And then I'm on my way.